HALF IN THE SUN

*For Chad,
with very best regards*

Thanks for listening,

Half IN THE Sun

ANTHOLOGY *of* MENNONITE WRITING

ELSIE K. NEUFELD
editor-in-chief

ROBERT MARTENS & LEONARD NEUFELDT
co-editors

LOUISE BERGEN PRICE &
MARYANN TJART JANTZEN
associate editors

RONSDALE PRESS

RONSDALE PRESS
3350 West 21st Avenue
Vancouver, B.C., Canada
V6S 1G7

Typesetting: Julie Cochrane, in New Baskerville 11 pt on 15
Cover Design: Marijke Friesen
Cover Image: Walter Neufeld
Paper: Rolland Enviro Cream (100% recycled)

Ronsdale Press wishes to thank the following for their support of its publishing program: the Canada Council for the Arts, the Government of Canada through the Book Publishing Industry Development Program (BPIDP), and the Province of British Columbia through the Book Publishing Tax Credit Program and the British Columbia Arts Council.

Library and Archives Canada Cataloguing in Publication

Half in the sun: anthology of Mennonite writing / Elsie K. Neufeld, editor-in-chief; Robert Martens & Leonard Neufeldt, co-editors; Louise Bergen Price & Maryann Tjart Jantzen, associate editors.

ISBN-13: 978-1-55380-038-5
ISBN-10: 1-55380-038-9

1. Canadian literature (English) — Mennonite authors. 2. Canadian literature (English) — British Columbia. 3. Canadian literature (English) — 20th century. I. Neufeld, Elsie K., 1957– II. Martens, Robert, 1949– III. Neufeldt, Leonard, 1937– IV. Price, Louise Bergen V. Jantzen, Maryann Tjart

PS8235.M4H34 2006   C810.8'09212897711   C2006-903186-X

At Ronsdale Press we are committed to protecting the environment. To this end we are working with Markets Initiative (www.oldgrowthfree.com) and printers to phase out our use of paper produced from ancient forests. This book is one step towards that goal.

Printed in Canada by Hignell Printing, Manitoba

You, standing half in the evening sun
and half in the shade wondering . . .
— LEONARD NEUFELDT

ACKNOWLEDGEMENTS

The production of this book would not have been possible without generous assistance. Funding has been provided by the Quiring-Loewen Trust; the Chilliwack Museum and Historical Society together with its affiliate, the Yarrow Research Committee; a donation in memory of Walter Klassen; a gift in memory of Jacob P. Martens; and an anonymous donation.

Books of this kind depend on the advice and encouragement of others. We are especially indebted to Patrick Friesen, Barbara Nickel and Andreas Schroeder, as well as to Ron Denman, Catherine McDonald and Joe Wiebe. For granting us a venue to feature many of the authors represented in this volume and promote its publication, we would like to thank the Mennonite Literary Society, its president, Garry Enns, and the editors of its nationally distributed magazine, *Rhubarb*.

We are also grateful to the authors included in this volume for their willingness to contribute texts and, in so doing, to help demonstrate the vitality of the community of Mennonite literary artists that has emerged on the West Coast in recent years.

The editors also wish to express special thanks to publisher Ronald B. Hatch for his faith in our anthology project.

CONTENTS

- Non-Fiction -

INTRODUCTION

Mennonites have a long history of profound commitment to their faith so that, from their founding in mid-sixteenth century Europe, impoverishment, suffering, and steady movement were their lot. They spread, over the years, through Switzerland, the Netherlands, Germany, Poland, Russia and Ukraine, to the United States, and finally into Canada, the earliest arriving here in the mid-eighteenth century, and more following well into the twentieth, until there are now more than one hundred thousand spread across our country. The Mennonite beliefs in adult baptism and in communal living, in pacifism, and living one's religion may have often set them at odds with their ruling governments and their neighbours, but at the same time, these beliefs also create close-knit, caring communities that provide a kind of physical and emotional security among its children otherwise hard to find in the modern Western world.

The writers who are represented in this anthology were all raised as Mennonites and share that troubled past and the beauty of the lived faith. They are all, regardless of where they were born, also today residents of British Columbia, so that we have something unique in this anthology: a mixture of the memory of the shared past, and of Canadian prairie farm and/or Mennonite village, and the damp, the rainforests, the mountains of B.C., and the vast and cosmopolitan city of Vancouver.

These stories and poems record the present that has grown out of the past: transformed as it often is, in men, into the ability to do and to love to do, for example, woodwork, things with the hands that fix and create the home and the shop, and for women, the garden, both vegetable and flower, and the tender, yet common-sensical caring for the one or two children — instead of the re-quired six or ten of the past — of the modern Canadian family. All of them learned early the necessity of work and are willing to do it; only some, helplessly, question work as a value in itself. Nearly all the writers included here drop Biblical references, pious say-ings of the church elders and of their parents or grandparents, and the oft-repeated teachings of childhood, often in the Low German in which originally they would have been said. Sometimes these are used with reverence, sometimes with humour, sometimes with a kind of head-shaking disbelief at such useless faith. But also with a hint of wonder that might be the deepest admiration.

The more traditional communities, though, turning their faces away from "progress" of all kinds, tended to ignite dissent in the breasts of some of their less conformist children. At its worst, as poet Robert Martens puts it in "a little mennonite goes a long way":

> . . . everyone could use a
> little mennonite at their side. dressed
> in black. hollow-eyed and tight-lipped.
> gloom pressing like anvils on his shoulders.
> recondite in homilies of grief . . .

The writers in this anthology are often torn between the two sides of the proverbial coin: the god, peace and home-loving simple ideals, and the too-tight rein kept on ideas and experience outside this realm. It is no wonder then, that today, the well-educated, prosperous, and sometimes faith-denying offspring of the Mennonites should turn to literature to express their very mixed feelings about both that past, and its influences on them, and the influence on them of the way the faith has been "lived," with the desire to tease out its meaning for the modern Canadian. These writers record and witness, laugh and sometimes weep, over the past that formed them. There are no stories of hate, or of rage at all the pleasure forbidden, lost and denied by such a faith, and only the occasional expression of bitterness; there is a sadness, a yearning for the beauty of the simple certainty left behind forever, for the honesty of it, and even for the pain such simple honesty brought or caused — the unimaginable suffering of the European past that cannot be denied, that must be assimilated by even the coolest teen, or the doctorate-owning, university-professor poet. And always with that unshakeable nostalgia for the imagined perfection of belief. How to use all of this? What to make of it? It is unlikely the answers to such questions will come from pastors or grandparents or history books. What is required is this — this anthology of first-rate poems and stories — where Mennonite artists struggle for meaning, for a truth, and to tell it *slant*. Give this to the children to read.

— Sharon Butala
March 29, 2006

Fiction

Renovating Heaven

- ANDREAS SCHROEDER -

The problem with the house that Father bought for us in Vancouver after we lost our farm in Agassiz wasn't so much that it was a wreck.

It was that he adamantly refused to let us do anything to fix it.

For weeks I pleaded and cajoled, offering to strip its peeling asbestos tiles or paint its decrepit window frames. I said I'd get an afterschool job and pay for the paint myself. I offered to dig up the weed-infested front yard and plant a proper lawn. I thought we could replace its trampled chickenwire fence with mill ends from a sawmill at the foot of Fraser Street.

Father showed some brief interest in the notion of a proper lawn, but even that, he explained, would have to wait. He had a plan, an integrated design, a vision for the whole place. There was no point in doing anything piecemeal. Things had to be done in the proper sequence.

Impatience just wasted money. There was no point in stripping the tiles when they'd only be torn off and replaced with stucco anyway. That wouldn't happen right away, of course; the interior would come first, the uneven floors, the rusted-out plumbing. There would be plenty for me to do just helping him replace the plaster-and-lath walls. If I had extra time on my hands, there'd be lots of studs to de-nail and the nails to straighten.

Getting ahead of ourselves would only cause more problems.

I rolled my eyes and appealed to Mother. She must have known there was no way I'd ever make any friends living in a shack like this. But Mother just shook her head. I couldn't really tell whose side she was on, but she knew better than to challenge Father once he had a plan. We all did.

And anyway, it wasn't the plan that was the problem. Father's plans usually made sense. This one certainly did. We all wanted a nice house. The problem was that Father's plans always took forever. They took a hundred million years.

"If that man had to build a box for no other reason than to carry a load of shit from the barn to the manure pile and then throw it away," I once overheard my Uncle Jakob grumble to Mother, "he'd still take a decade and build it to rival the Ark of the Covenant. That man's incapable of building for less than eternity, Margarete." Uncle Jakob had been waiting for his promised bathroom cabinet for over a year. "He's got the cart before the horse. Eternity comes *after* life on earth — and I was planning to live them in that order!"

It wasn't even that I didn't understand Father's point of view. Mother had already explained it to me several times. After searching for almost half a year for a job in Vancouver, Father had finally found one at the MacDonald Sash & Door Company. The Mac-Donald Sash & Door Company didn't actually make doors, it made wooden ladders, but the point was, Father was finally going to be working with wood again. His training in cabinetry was going to be utilized once more. Deep down he'd always hated farming.

But making ladders the Canadian way had turned out to be a huge disappointment. "They slap those things together like the worst kind of junk," he'd reported to Mother after his first day at work. "Rotten wood, splintery dowels, no bolts, everything just stiffened with cheap glue. A year in a damp shed and it'd fall apart the first time you stepped on it!"

Even at age ten I already knew what that meant. In our house, sloppiness was next to Godlessness. Father talked about sloppiness the way Elder Friesen talked about mortal sin.

So our house, Mother had explained to me, was going to be Father's answer to the MacDonald Sash & Door Company. Or actually, his answer to Canada. Every line would be plumb. Every angle would be precise. The floors would be so perfectly level that a marble wouldn't know which way to roll. It would be Father's "triumph and absolution," she said. I nodded sadly. I didn't really understand what she meant by triumph and absolution but I had a pretty good idea how long they would take to achieve. And with his job, Father would only be able to renovate evenings and weekends.

I contemplated rebellion and insurrection. I fantasized buying five-gallon pails of paint and slathering the entire exterior on a weekend when Father wasn't home. I imagined organizing a work party of my friends, transfiguring the front yard in a gardening *blitzkrieg*. I knew it would all be temporary — wasteful and sinful — a fake facade over imprecision and corruption, but I didn't care. I was prepared to answer for that. Anything was better than having to live the rest of my life in this embarrassing hovel.

But my fantasies never progressed past the imagining stage. I hadn't yet made any friends in this city, and anyway, Father never went away for weekends.

—

Mother had promised Heidi that when we moved to the city, we'd still have a big garden. (With a big garden we'd still qualify as farmers and could still get to heaven.) But this garden also fell victim to Father's master plan. There'd be a garden eventually, certainly, but it would have to wait until the garage was torn down, and for the moment there were more important things on Father's list than tearing down the garage. So Mother suggested we keep a couple of rabbits instead.

Father was dubious, but Gutrun was delighted and Heidi was ecstatic. I was delegated to build the rabbit hutch, so I was also pleased. It gave me a legitimate reason to use Father's tools — something he rarely permitted. It also gave me a legitimate reason to tear down the front yard fence — I'd need that chickenwire for the rabbit run. I was pretty sure Father wouldn't spring for new chickenwire.

It turned out I was right on all counts. Clearly, Father was really preoccupied. He barely looked up from his drawings and measurements when I made off with his sledgehammer and crowbar. He didn't supervise my attack on the back wall of the garage for a supply of boards for the hutch. He virtually ignored me as I rummaged around in his nail supply for shingle nails.

I finished the hutch about a week later. It looked great to me. I'd taken considerable pains with the measuring and cutting, and had even used a right-angle to make everything square. The rabbit run was a narrow wire corridor about ten feet long, framed with old studs and separated from the hutch by a guillotine door. Heidi could barely contain herself.

"Is that where they'll go for their picnics?" she demanded, her little body bobbing and squirming with excitement. "Is that where they'll have their races?"

Even Father seemed impressed. He pointed out only four things I'd gotten wrong. After that he asked me where I'd left his fencing pliers and his level. He said there wasn't much point in owning tools if you could never find them. Fortunately Gutrun found them right inside the hutch where they hadn't gotten wet. That was the only place I hadn't looked.

If I'd had any idea how much trouble they would get me into over the next couple of months, I'd never have offered to find us the rabbits. I also hadn't realized how hard it would be to find them in a city. In Agassiz it would have been a simple matter of asking around at school. A lot of local people kept rabbits, and somebody was always giving some away. But at our school in Vancouver I couldn't find anyone who knew of any rabbits. I asked around church too, with no better luck.

Then somebody suggested laundromats.

I'd never heard of laundromats, but there were several on Fraser Street so I began to monitor their bulletin boards. And sure enough, about three weeks later I saw an announcement: THREE CHINCHILLA GRAY TICKED RABBITS, ONE MALE, TWO FEMALE, FREE TO GOOD HOME, 499 East 55th Avenue. The address was only about six blocks from our place.

"Oh yeah, these'll give you plenty of excitement," the man who answered the door chuckled, pulling one out of its cage. He looked like Deacon Doerksen with his bald head and rimless glasses. The rabbit looked awfully big. "Regular little Houdinis, these rascals. Did you bring a box?"

I hadn't. Actually, I'd only meant to have a look and then report back. But everything just seemed to happen without stopping. Ten minutes later I was walking up Prince Edward Street with a box full of three struggling rabbits.

"Guess what I've got," I said to Heidi when I got home. The rabbits in the box thumped and scratched. Heidi's eyes became huge. "We've got rabbits, we've got rabbits," she shrieked, trying to thrust her fingers into the box. Mother came in from the kitchen; Father came up from the basement. I opened the box carefully, keeping the flaps upright so the rabbits wouldn't jump out.

"The notice in the laundromat said they were Chinchillas, but the man called them Houdinis," I said. Father actually laughed. Mother smiled. "What?" I demanded. Father said Houdini had been a famous escape artist in the '20s. Even Mennonites knew about him. He said I'd better make sure my hutch was really escape-proof. Heidi looked worried.

"They'll never get out of that hutch," I assured her. "How could they possibly get through all that wood and wire?"

We asked ourselves that very question the next morning when we found the hutch empty and the rabbits gone.

Father pointed to a hole they'd burrowed under the frame of the run. He said I'd probably have to set the run on a brick or stone foundation.

I found the rabbits munching grass in the ditch that ran along our back alley. I caught the first two fairly easily, but it took me an hour to get the third safely back into the hutch. I didn't let them out into their run until I'd built a brick foundation under its frame.

The next day they were gone again. This time they'd found and stretched a small gap in the chickenwire.

I closed the gap and recaptured them. They got out again two days later by chewing through a wooden slat. A week later they knocked out a knot in a board and enlarged the hole. I can't remember how they got out the next time, or the next, or the next. No matter how much I strengthened, fortified and reinforced their cage, they kept finding ways to get out.

"They're regular escape artists all right," Mother said, smiling. Heidi laughed. "That one there's Hootie," she said. "And that one's Tootie. He's the worstest one." Gutrun grinned. Everybody seemed to find this escaping business funny except me. I was the one who always had to chase after them.

Eventually I did start gaining on our Houdinis. Their escapes dropped from every few days to every few weeks. I buried the chickenwire more than a foot deep all around their run and even covered the hutch with it. I found some more old bricks and paved their entire run bottom. I attached a spring to their hutch door and put a lock on it.

That August our next-door neighbour at number 430, Mr. Henry Windebank, stopped by to talk to Father. He wanted to discuss the fence between our houses. It was in sorry shape and needed replacing. He reminded Father that every property owner was responsible for the fence on his west side. He said he was planning to have his yard landscaped and his old lawn replaced, and he hoped Father would consider replacing the fence at the same time.

I don't think Father knew about being responsible for our west-side fence and I suspected it wasn't very high on his renovation list, but I could see that he didn't want to have a fight with Mr. Windebank. So we spent the following Saturday digging out crumbling fenceposts and smashing apart the sections in-between. For the rest of the week, from after school until it got dark, I got to burn the piles of rotten boards we'd heaped up along the property line, which I enjoyed, and I finished the job by the next weekend like I'd promised, although on one of the days Mrs. Windebank got upset about the smoke dirtying the washing on her clothesline, which I hadn't noticed.

And then the summer ended a bit more quickly than anyone expected, which meant Mr. Windebank's new lawn didn't really get a chance to green up before the fall rains started, and pretty soon everything was sopping wet and muddy. The runoff cut crooked little creeks all over our backyard, and after a while I had to jump from rock to rock to take the garbage to our garbage can in the back alley.

I was in the middle of doing my English homework in the diningroom when Heidi burst in, not even taking off her boots or raincoat. "It's Hootie," she gasped, waving a broken stick that sprayed water drops all over my books. "She's gotten out, and that dog from across the street is chasing her!"

I didn't stop to ask questions. The terrier from the family that had recently moved into number 431 had immediately become the scourge of the neighbourhood, knocking over garbage cans, scattering garbage, chasing everybody's cats and dogs. As I raced outside I caught sight of him just disappearing around the back of our house. I gave chase, but only managed to catch up because they reversed somewhere in the backyard and came high-tailing back.

By this time Hootie had given up trying to hide and was just trying to outrace the dog. At the sight of me standing directly in her path she shot almost two feet into the air, made the most amazing mid-air turn, and was churning away at a perfect right angle, her back feet throwing up a spray of mud and pebbles almost before she hit the ground. The terrier tried changing direction just as fast but he lost traction and skidded wide. I charged after Hootie, trying my best to keep her madly bobbing tail in view. The terrier was coming up fast from behind.

I don't remember when the thought struck me that something was terribly wrong. I'd been so intent on the chase that I'd paid no attention to where it was going. I ran three or four more steps and then stopped. Hootie disappeared. The terrier rushed past me and disappeared. I was left standing in the middle of Mr. Windebank's freshly sown lawn, up to my knees in churned-up mud.

Behind me a brutally stark line of deeply punched footsteps led back across the lawn, over the property line and into my own back yard. The evidence couldn't have been more incriminating.

I made a few half-hearted attempts to fill in the nearest hole, but that just increased the damage. I tried to turn around by stepping into the already existing holes, but the pattern was maddeningly reversed. Now my right foot was on the wrong side of my body, and my left foot wouldn't fit into my right footprint. It was hopeless.

I looked over at Mr. Windebank's house but his curtains were motionless. I looked over toward my house, expecting to see the same. What I saw instead was Father, standing large as life in the middle of our livingroom window. The expression on his face was terrifying.

As I made another move to retrace my steps he yanked open the side window. "Stop!" he ordered, aiming a devastating finger down at me. "Don't move! I'm coming down."

I stood there paralyzed, listening to his thundering footsteps on the stairs.

But when he arrived and looked the situation over, there wasn't much he could do. I kept trying to step into my former footsteps, but even when I managed one, the hole became a lot bigger. By the time I'd made it back, it looked as if I'd dragged a stoneboat or a cow carcass across the Windebank lawn.

Father just shook his head. "Get yourself cleaned up," was all he said.

By the time I'd cleaned my boots and returned upstairs, Father had sized the situation up, and it looked grim. Windebank would sue us within an inch of our lives. We wouldn't be able to pay, and we'd probably lose the house. Or we'd be in debt to lawyers forever after. Once those carnivores got their claws into you, Father said, they never let go. Everyone knew that. Falling into the hands of officials or bureaucrats was more dangerous than falling into the clutches of the Antichrist. Why on earth had he ever agreed to let us have those *verflixte* rabbits in the first place?

I offered, timidly, to go apologize to Mr. Windebank.

"Apologize?" Father snorted. "Of course you should apologize. But that's not going to make any difference. Apologies don't make the slightest difference once lawyers are involved."

And the more Father thought about it, the worse the scenario became. Once we'd been sued in court, he realized we'd have a criminal record, and once we had a record, our bid for Canadian citizenship was out the window. How likely was it that Canada would grant citizenship to people with a criminal record? Not a chance, that's what. All our hopes and dreams for a new start in a civilized country — right out the window. And why? All because he'd foolishly agreed to let us have a bunch of *verfluchte* rabbits.

"I'll go apologize to Mr. Windebank right now," I said, pulling on my raincoat. "Maybe then he won't sue us and take away our house."

I rang Mr. Windebank's doorbell about a hundred times, but there was nobody home.

By the time I got back to our house, Father's take on our situation had reached catastrophic levels. It wasn't just a matter of not getting our citizenship. It was a lot worse than that. He had just realized that once we had a criminal record, we would be subject to deportation. That's what they did with landed immigrants who fell afoul of the law. He remembered an emigration officer warning us about that back in Hamburg. We'd be sent back on the *Beaverbrae*, straight back to Germany, which wouldn't want us, had never wanted us because we were pacifists, and now, with a criminal record, would definitely not want to have anything to do with us. And then where would we go? We'd probably spend the rest of our lives as Displaced Persons in some hopeless refugee camp in Prussia or Poland.

And all because he hadn't had the foresight to get rid of those *verdammte* English rabbits!

"I'll go out and see if Mr. Windebank's back home yet," I said, hurriedly putting my raincoat back on. "Maybe he's gotten back home already."

He wasn't, but I didn't have the courage to go home and listen to Father anymore. I just stood out on our porch and watched the Windebanks' house for about three hours. I thought I'd see them walking up their sidewalk and then I'd apologize, but finally their front light came on so I guess they must have driven in from the back. I rushed over to their front door and pushed the doorbell, but when the door opened and Mr. Windebank was standing there, I got so confused, I talked to him in German. *"Den Rasen,"* I said, pointing desperately into the dark. *"Ich hab' euren Rasen kaputt gemacht. Es tut mir schrecklich leid."*

"What's he saying?" Mrs. Windebank asked, coming up behind her husband. I kept pointing.

"Why is that boy crying, Henry?"

Mr. Windebank had already looked in the direction I was pointing. "Did your rabbits get out again, Peter?" he asked, shading his eyes against the porchlight. He didn't sound terribly angry. "Well, we'll have to do a little patching after the grass grows back in, that's clear, but there's not much point doing anything until spring. Too wet right now. Too muddy." He clapped me good-humouredly on the shoulder. "Nothing to get all upset about, my lad. Not the end of the world. We'll wait for spring." He turned me around and aimed me back toward our house. "You be sure to tell your parents hello from me now, you hear?"

For a moment I just stood there stunned, staring wildly up into his eyes. Then I bounded home like a rabbit chased by a terrier. As I yanked off my raincoat I could hear Father talking in the kitchen to Mother. He was telling her to phone Pastor Driediger at the Mennonite Brethren Church. He said those Mennonite Brethren were far more likely to have lawyers in their congregation than our

Mennonite Conference. He wanted her to write to Uncle Jakob too, because Uncle Jakob understood the deviousness of Canadian criminal and citizenship law.

"It's okay, Father!" I shouted from the doorway. "It's all right! Mr. Windebank isn't going to sue!"

"Don't interrupt, Peter," Father said tiredly. "You've caused enough trouble for one day already. Margarete, if you think the mail might be too slow, we might have to telephone Jakob tomorrow."

"But Father! I apologized to Mr. Windebank! I apologized, and Mr. Windebank said it was okay."

"Did you hear him, Gerhard?" Mother said, sounding anxious.

"Did I hear what?"

"Mr. Windebank isn't going to sue," I said. "I talked to him, and he isn't going to sue."

"Who's not suing?" Father demanded.

"Mr. Windebank."

Father looked exasperated. "And how would you know a thing like that?"

"I just talked to him."

"What? When?"

"A few minutes ago. He said he wasn't going to sue."

There was a long silence, or so it seemed to me, and then Father pulled over a chair and sat down. He sat down like a sack of potatoes, as if all the strength had gone out of him. He didn't say anything; he just sat there staring at Mother's hands in an unfocussed way. And the strange thing was, I couldn't tell whether he was relieved or disappointed.

Finally he turned to me. "He said that, did he? Are you sure that's what he said?"

"Yes, Father."

"You're sure you didn't misunderstand?"

"No, Father."

"Because those English, when they start talking fast, you can never be sure exactly what they're saying."

I tried hard not to forget what Mr. Windebank had said.

"He said it wasn't time for the end of the world yet."

Father snorted. "I suppose he *has* to hope that's true."

He didn't move for a while longer, and then he shrugged thoughtfully. "Well, at least that gives us some breathing room," he said. He got up slowly, almost painfully. "Because you never know about the English. They'll say that one day, and then the very next . . ."

Mother and I watched his back disappearing down the basement stairs.

Mother turned back to the sink and resumed washing her pots. "So Mr. Windebank said it wasn't time for the world to end?"

Her voice was gentle. I couldn't tell whether she was relieved or alarmed.

I nodded. "Maybe not until spring. He said it wouldn't be the end of the world until the spring."

Ashes

- DARCIE FRIESEN HOSSACK -

Libby would rather be in the garden. It's almost warm enough this April, with teasings of green having arrived on the land to predict an early spring. She doesn't need the signs of seasonal shift for her to feel a winter's worth of longing — the desire to walk with bare feet through warm mud. Indeed, she imagines herself taking root alongside seeds harvested from last year's best squash and melons. She will plant tomatoes as well, although she has sometimes been charged with giving them too much space in the garden, space that could otherwise be seeded with more sensible vegetables. Vegetables in straight rows with modest coverings of husks and pods and rinds. Or potatoes, ugly but underground.

Tomatoes make Anke nervous. The way they become vulnerable to every whim of weather at the first hint of ripening. The way their soft flesh yields to the slightest pressure, their gel-enveloped seeds. There was a time when she used to pick and eat them in the afternoon, when they were warm on the vine. Now she presses them into sterilized jars instead, tempers their sweetness with a boiling salt-and-vinegar brine.

Besides tomato red there are other colours Anke finds disturbing. Blue, like the scattered shards of cobalt pottery seeded through the back garden. And yellow. Tuscany yellow. The name of a paint she'd once chosen for one of the bedrooms.

Unlike Libby, Anke is a sure voice for practicality. But, since Matthew went and married Libby anyway, Anke won't say a word to him about it now. Tell him that girls like Libby inevitably come to grief. That their careless, barefoot-in-the-spring ways, their enthusiasm, undoes them. And Anke's not willing to explain how she knows this.

"It's been so warm. Almost like home on the coast," Libby says to Anke, even though she knows that referring so often to the landscape of her life before Saskatchewan may irritate Anke. "I saw Meryl next door putting out stakes for her sweet peas."

"Meryl?" Anke repeats, as though she has never heard the name.

"Mrs. Larsen's daughter-in-law. Remember? There were such lovely peonies at Jake and Meryl's wedding last summer. All different pinks. I'm thinking of trying to hybridize a new variety to name after Meryl." Libby knows Anke wishes she would attach herself to the daughters of Anke's friends rather than their daughters-in-law.

"What I know is that you sure-as-sin don't want anyone to think of you in the same breath as that senseless Meryl," Anke says. "I went to pay her a visit after she moved in over there, you know, and found her popping pansies into her mouth like she was eating lettuce. And acting as though there was nothing at all strange about it. Why would you want to name a flower . . ." Her voice trails off as she sees Libby heaping fruit into a pie shell.

"Libby. You'll be using up the last of my good peaches on just one pie if you keep that up. I want to keep at least six to put in the freezer. And besides, it just doesn't seem right somehow to pile fruit all up on top of itself like that."

Anke bites her tongue to keep from delivering a short sermon on "immoral fruit." Libby will have to learn to curb her tendencies for excess, she thinks.

Libby sighs, spoons most of the macerated fruit from the pie shell back into the bowl, and spreads the thin layer of remaining peaches over the bottom crust before putting on the top crust. She crimps the edges and wonders when Anke learned to be so tight. Even sleep seems a necessity Anke resents when there is work that could be done instead. But Libby, as she sits by the kitchen window while she works on the peaches, is in a good mood, preferring peace on such a lovely day when everything outside seems filled with possibilities and secrets and seeds. She smoothes a hand over the small new curve under her apron and smiles.

"There's no need for showing that off," Anke says, noticing Libby's fingers moving under the pleated, curtain-like fabric tied at her waist. She had lately presented Libby with a set of seven such aprons, one for each day and a special one for Sunday. In case they should be surprised in the kitchen by neighbours, she explained, or the nosey farm boy hired to help in the fields this year. "I myself stayed out of sight when young and expecting," she adds. "But I suppose things were different then . . . even in cities . . ."

Libby from the city. Anke sighs, forgetting for a moment that she's not alone. Libby, with her college degree in plants and no sense of how fickle they can be, especially on the prairies. Libby, who Anke believes vexed Anke's husband into his grave last summer with all her organic ideas and hybrid seeds and bulbs. He might have lived another year, she suspects, if not pressed to change his ways. But Anke never brings that up, either. How, as a widow, she had no choice but to sell her house to her son and let Libby behave as though it was her own to do with as she pleases — while Anke lives like an unwelcome guest in the upstairs bedroom, pretending tiredness at seven-thirty in the evening so she isn't in their way. Do they appreciate her sacrifice? It doesn't matter, she tells herself; generosity should be performed without thought of rewards awaiting her in heaven.

And soon, God willing, there will be an infant and what a chore that will be, to undo all the permissive upbringing and unchecked affection she's sure the child will receive. So, although she has lately begun to feel pain in her chest when it is cold and in her head when it is hot, she is determined to live long enough to see that her grandchild isn't raised without some good German sense.

"I've been thinking about a name for the child," Anke announces. "Abraham. After *his* grandfather. It only seems right."

"I don't think we want to name a baby after someone who's dead," Libby replies too quickly. "And, besides, we think it's a girl."

"There's never been a girl born first in my family."

It's not entirely true. Not true at all, in fact. There was her little Ruth, but too few people remember her. And now Libby's quick refusal to consider the name has injured Anke, and she imagines how her son must have been manipulated into agreeing to forget his father. The same way he was seduced into marrying this girl who, with all her untried ideas about farming, is practically a foreigner. She knows she should have insisted, insisted harder, that he go to school in Saskatchewan. Only nonsense comes from wanting to live by the ocean. And Libby is all nonsense, unlike the girls he would have met in Saskatoon or Regina. Steady girls, with parents who know where they've come from.

Libby considers herself a "Canadian," as if saying so means anything. An Irish-Italian mother and a mostly Dutch father. Who can even keep track of such genetic clutter?

"How about Abel?" Libby compromises.

"So, you won't use the name of my dead husband," Anke says evenly, again *not* sinking into accusations, "but you'll curse a child with the name of the first person murdered on this earth."

"I just thought . . ."

"What? That it's almost like Abraham? I'm sure in your mind it is."

Libby considers suggesting Jezebel for a girl, but decides it won't make either of them feel better.

"And don't go thinking up any of those new-age names you west-coast girls are so infatuated with. I won't have a grandchild named Summer or Apple or God knows what else. A solid European name is best in Saskatchewan. German, since that's what he'll be."

Anke wants to say the name Ruth, but it sticks in her throat like a stone, and she swallows hard to force it back down.

The kitchen is too hot, the oven breathing out heat for the baking of Anke's half-inch thick pies. Although Libby knows what thoughts it will prompt in her mother-in-law's mind, she slips outside through the kitchen's back door, where she breathes in slow draughts of spring air, testing it for substance like a vintner pondering young wine for a sense of its emerging notes of oak and florals. This will be her third summer here, so far away from the mountains and mild coastal weather. Where farming takes place in occasional valleys, not all over the province, on expansive fields flat as an unspooled carpet. Like here. Here, where her wedding to Matthew, like everything else, had waited for the harvest.

And then came the shock of her first real winter, when the temperature on the thermometer meant nothing if there was wind. And there was always wind.

It was during a wintertime walk, when she went out into what began as a soft, insulating snowfall but changed suddenly into a blizzard whipping the snow sideways and freezing the moisture in her lungs, that Libby had found an abandoned outbuilding at the far edge of the farm.

With a small wood-burning stove and a stack of dry wood and matches, Libby had been able to make a fire and keep warm until the storm passed. And then later, in the spring, she claimed and restored it into a haven for herself and her plants. A place, she also imagined, for her children to play. Two girls and a boy is what she hopes for, and she dreams of them planting their own corner of garden with seeds for red and yellow carrots and candy cane beets. Chasing one another on the freshly cut grass, stopping to sing "Ring Around The Rosy." Tumbling down, laughing, after *ashes, ashes.*

We all fall down, Libby sings, thinking of Anke and wondering why she had had only one child. She has often thought a daughter might have softened Anke.

Although Anke had only mentioned it once, she had disapproved from the outset of Libby's plans for the shed. Strangely possessive of a place she never visited, Libby thought. But because Anke kept her disdain quiet and distant, Libby swished up cobwebs and pushed dust out the door in what felt like her first true act of housekeeping. Now the walls are hung with new shelves of old wood displaying her collection of glass cloches — from tiny domes that warm the most delicate young sprouts to giant mute bells that serve as a surrogate sun to tomatoes. Libby thinks of the cloches as silent keepers of garden memory; she believes in their ability to remember plants. The same way a woman's body remembers its children.

Libby has walked further than she meant to, her feet finding the path to the shed. It always seems to happen like this when she has let her mind wander, the shed coming into view unexpectedly, rewarding her with the comforting sight of its weathered plank walls and gentle windward lean.

I wonder what these walls remember? Libby muses as she steps up into their shade. She touches the lintel as if to remind the shed of who she is.

When she first found the shed that winter, it had contained nothing but a packet of unviable poppy seeds and a few clay pots, now filled with fragments of blue pottery she'd found everywhere in the shed's adjoining small square of garden. The shards told her that the shed and its garden hadn't always been a secret, though it's impossible to know when it was last used. But Libby knows that if the shards had been left in the garden, their sharp edges would have threatened the roots of tomatoes and pansies and, even if the plants survived, they'd be unable to bloom.

From inside the shed, which she's scrubbed and scrubbed, the old, sunken glass windows, etched and altered by decades of dust storms, will never be clear. When Libby looks through them, the world appears as if under water, the way she imagines it would be if she could watch the world through someone else's eyes.

For all its silent suggestions of former use and ownership, Libby feels the old garden shed has begun to accept her, a transplant, struggling to thrive among sturdier stalks. Still, the shed seems determined to keep its secrets.

In the kitchen, Anke — though she prefers being left alone to do things the right way, the right way the first time — is working herself into satisfied indignation over Libby's absence. Where is that girl, anyway? She should want to be here. To help. To learn through practice and Anke's instruction how women in Anke's family do things. And that includes learning how to take care of Anke's son the way he's been used to.

Such a dear boy, she says to herself. For all his soft-heartedness and lack of sense. But she can't blame him for that. It was Libby who took advantage and then didn't know her place. It was Libby who made him think he should come in from the fields and still have to do more. Like clearing the table or wiping his crumbs off the counter or rinsing the bar of soap when he's dirtied it. Such little things. It would be easier for Libby to do them herself rather than always nag. So when Anke notices the soap is covered in muddy bubbles that puddle the sink's crackled porcelain, she gives it all a rinse. There, you see? She has flushed dissent down the drain by doing the chore herself.

Anke knows her pies are done by the particular aroma of hot fruit. Years of baking have given her a sense about such things, a knack that once allowed her to keep a sparse, uncluttered kitchen. Now there are drawers full of new gadgets. A bouquet of whisks when one fork would do. Timers and thermometers for everything, when Anke can throw together a six-course meal and bring it to the table just as everyone suddenly realizes they're hungry. All without looking at a clock.

And that's another thing. Libby has a clock for every room and always wears a watch, constantly checking to make sure they're all set at the exact same time. As if the world revolves around those clocks instead of the other way around. Anke has woken up every day for fifty years at 5:15 a.m., and she doesn't need anyone to wake her or tell her the time.

Lost in her thoughts of Libby, Anke has whipped cream most of the way into butter. Her favourite fork for the task lashes deftly through the thickening foam, the sound of it changing, becoming dull as its volume increases in her mother's old enamelled bowl, chipped by two generations of everyday use. She won't add sugar or vanilla to *her* cream. No need for such extravagance. Especially on a Tuesday.

Outside, Libby watches as a robin settles on a fence post and shuffles its wings into place, its red breast pushed out to announce its springtime intentions. She remembers a time when she discovered a chick fallen from its twig-and-fluff nest littered with broken blue egg shells. The chick was dead. Naked and vulnerable. Its featherless wings splayed as if ready for flight, while, above, its squawking siblings in the nest were aware only of worms being thrust into their open mouths.

"The world is cruel like that," Libby says to the robin. It cocks its head and looks at her closely with one dark eye, then the other. Anke would say the same. About the world being cruel. Except she wouldn't stop along her way to feel sorrow. *Nothing is safe until it's dead,* is how she'd put it. Libby had buried the chick beneath the tree and placed a stone on its grave.

Inside of her, Libby's baby is still, when only yesterday she had felt it flutter its limbs. But, she reminds herself, the doctor had assured her last week that a bit of blood wasn't much to worry about. So long as there wasn't more. And there hadn't been.

"You shouldn't get too attached before it's time," Anke had told her, but Libby was fully committed from the moment in the bathroom when she'd held the wand and watched it turn blue. Blue for *positive.* That was more than fourteen weeks ago.

"Do you feel that?" Libby says. She touches her belly, but there is no response. She lifts her face to the sun, feels her skin grow warm. *Are you asleep?* As when the lights go out in a storm, she struggles to sense the outline of something that recently seemed so clear. But it won't come to her, and instead she tries to remember what it was that had driven her out of the kitchen.

"No point trying to help now," Anke says without looking up from a sink full of dishes. "Just change out of that dusty dress before supper. And if you can manage that, then set the table. You may as well know I've invited Mrs. Larsen and her son from next door. Seems his new wife went to visit her mother."

"Is Meryl's mother all right?" Libby asks, but Anke continues as if Libby hasn't spoken.

"I don't know what that girl was thinking, going off with nothing at all made to eat. Old Mrs. Larsen isn't the woman, or the cook, she used to be."

Old Mrs. Larsen's only problem is that she's sour, Libby is tempted to answer, thinking of the woman's miserly, puckered face. Small wonder Anke is her most faithful friend. Libby pushes the thought aside, concentrating instead on a wave of fatigue and the feeling — as if something that's been leaking out of her slowly has suddenly drained away. She feels something new. Working its way into pain.

"I'll set the table, Anke. But I'm going to eat later. I'm not feeling very well," Libby says. The thought of sitting down to supper with the pair of condescending old ladies makes her head feel light and sick as though she's been thrown suddenly sideways. *The doctor said not to worry*, she reminds herself again. But was that really what he'd said? Right now she remembers only hearing her child's heart beating for the first time. The cold tape across her belly, measuring a new pound of progress.

"And what excuse shall I make for you?" Anke asks, provoked by the scent of outdoors on Libby's clothes. "No, you'll sit and eat with us. You can rest once our company's gone."

Libby sighs. She feels vacant, has to stop to count on her fingers how many plates and how many forks she needs to complete her task.

"Call me when they come," Libby says without looking back. She examines her face in the bathroom mirror. It seems featureless. As though her eyes and mouth and nose need to be pencilled in. She gives in to a compelling need to sit down.

Too much sun, she says to herself, letting the coolness of the tiled floor catch her slowly. Such a beautiful blue. She's always thought the mosaic, with its patterns of cerulean and cobalt, its reliefs of yellow, a strange choice for Anke, when everything else in the house is so plain. Her husband once told her it was his mother's own design, but this is the first time she's thought the tiles familiar in another way. In a way that refuses to become clear to her now as she tries to make sense of a resonating ache, an inward physical agony that is both pain and grief.

She follows the pain with both hands, from the rise of her belly down between the cradle of her hips to her pelvis and beneath the sturdy elastic of her new maternity underwear, where her fingers find the blood, warm and sticky and thick.

"Anke!" she calls, too softly at first, her voice growing louder and higher-pitched in each wave of pain that pauses only to surge through her back until it seems she will crack open. Like a gourd splitting in the sun to spill its seeds. She leans and slides into the discharge.

"What's this?" Anke asks at the door. "What are you doing down there?" She steps closer, trying to see what Libby is staring at. Why she's curled on the cold floor, her fingers exploring the tiles.

Libby looks up and then back down. She lifts a bloodied hand and begins to cry. She presses her wrists to her forehead, her soiled fingers staining her hair red.

"Oh," Anke says. She lets out her breath slowly, unable to find other words when she finally sees blood on the floor, a shallow stain spreading out from underneath Libby. She should have known. Had known. Had *chosen* to ignore her intuition. The way she herself had known when they sent her daughter home, saying the fever which was present before her fall and the blood from her nose that stopped only to start again were not unusual symptoms for a two-year-old. *A bug and a bump*; that's how the doctor had referred to it. And assured Anke that such *typical childhood incidents* would, in the end, make the girl stronger.

"Well, I suppose it wasn't meant to be. And you're not the first to . . ." Anke doesn't finish the sentence. She reaches under the sink for the stack of old towels. She presses a cold wet cloth into Libby's hands and bends to examine her, finding the lifeless form in the puddle between Libby's trembling legs.

With a pair of scissors taken from Libby's bathroom drawer, Anke severs the link between mother and child and lifts the tiny, doll-like baby into her palm — a girl, just as Libby had predicted. She reaches above her to the sink and wets a cloth with warm water, then gently begins to wipe blood away from the tiny forehead and eyelids, on eyes that will never open. Arms and legs too fragile to handle with her own, suddenly thick, clumsy hands. She counts the baby's fingers and toes.

"She's perfect, Libby," Anke says. She is about to lift the baby where Libby can see, but just then Libby has another contraction, is thrust into another spasm of pain.

"It's almost over," Anke says, tenderly placing her granddaughter on a soft towel and covering her with a washcloth. She takes Libby's hand.

After Libby's womb has emptied itself, Anke helps her into bed. "I'll call the doctor and ask if there's anything else we should do," Anke says, her voice falling as she remembers that they're still expecting company and it will be up to her to make the necessary excuses. "And I'll tell the Larsens you've had a bit of a headache from being outside," she adds. "No sense them knowing everything that goes on around here."

She sets a glass of water and an aspirin on the nightstand next to Libby and stops before going back to the kitchen to arrange more towels under her just in case. "There's still cooking to finish," she says abruptly, as though surprised, and then continues quietly, "but I'll see to that myself."

When Matthew comes in from the field, Anke is carrying a mop and a bucket full of chemical-smelling water towards the bathroom. She had hoped to have it clean before he came, so he wouldn't overreact, but he has surprised her by being early, and now there is nothing to do but tell him what happened. "I'm sorry, I would have come to find you," she adds when his questions become accusing, "but I'd have had to leave Libby alone. The doctor has been here and will see Libby again in the morning."

Anke lets him go and remains in the bathroom doorway long after he's gone to be with Libby. *Another father too late for the death of his daughter.* Anke stares at her beautiful blue tiles, smeared once again with blood. She knows the ceramic tiles won't stain. Even the broken ones, scattered like ashes behind the shed, remain true to their colour.

"Libby at least had me," Anke says to herself. She touches her face, surprised to find it wet with tears. As it had been when Anke, a young wife, was alone and afraid, and it was Ruth's blood pooling on the mosaic floor, streaming into the runnels of grout, where it clotted and dried. Later, she had begged her husband to tear up the floor, but he had insisted on simply scrubbing it clean with bleach. That's when all her intentions for improving the house were put away. After Ruth's death, she would allow only the least of what was necessary. Sturdy, practical fittings and drab colours. None of the sunny Tuscan yellows or saturated blues she loved. No red. Only beige, the colour of old wax.

But the tiles remained, reminding her of how much could be lost if she cared too much. In truth, she had been glad to move upstairs last summer, where there were fewer memories. Little to remind her of anything. Especially not of the daughter who had made her think in colours.

"The world is cruel like that," Anke says, stiffening herself so she can welcome her guests. But now, her thin peach pie seems merely stingy, not sensible. And Old Mrs. Larsen looks just old.

Anke hesitates, removes a plate from the table, suddenly glad that Libby has always had more sense than to listen to her pessimism. *Life shouldn't go back to normal until she's been able to spend her grief,* Anke thinks. "Olivia won't be joining us," she informs her guests. "She's not well, so of course I've told her to rest."

—

Libby has not slept. Not even with the prescription Matthew picked up while she waited in the car. The pills make her feel vague, not sleepy. She has lain awake two nights in a row watching her husband sleep. *How could a man, a father,* she wonders, *bury his child and then bury the grief of it in sleep?* But without anyone to answer, she listens to the noises the house makes. Noises that until now she has never noticed. Its old bones settling like sighs. Like Anke, who so often sighs before withdrawing into silence.

Libby hears Anke's feet touch the floor upstairs and knows it's 5:15 a.m. without looking at the clock. She expects to hear her mother-in-law next in the kitchen, lighting the stove for coffee, and dropping a slice of bread in the toaster. But instead, Libby hears the shush of the bedroom door being pushed over the carpet.

A long moment passes before Anke says, "Libby? I need to show you something." She knows without asking that her daughter-in-law is awake. Otherwise, Anke wouldn't have come.

Libby wraps herself in the mud-brown velour robe Matthew gave her last year for Christmas. The one Anke had picked out from the Sears catalogue and ordered, as always, without first asking her son.

Outside, pale yellow light has steeped the horizon in the exact shade of camomile tea. The colour and stillness of the hour and the fresh morning moisture on her face surprise Libby.

The women walk side-by-side, Anke carefully guiding Libby, and Libby allowing herself to be led as if drawn by a string.

"I thought it would disappear with enough time," Anke says quietly, stopping in front of the potting shed. In the early light, it looks restored. Not new, but fresh, as though well-rested after a night of good dreams.

"I used to love walking down to this shed. It was the one place that felt like my own. I thought my daughter and I would share it . . ."

"Daughter?"

Anke nods and draws in a breath. "Ruth wasn't even two when we lost her. Afterwards, I tried to forget her. I thought I was supposed to. But forgetting someone completely takes even more stubbornness than I have."

Anke looks at the shed and all the life brought back to it. Like a grave someone's tended after long neglect.

"There's blue pottery in the garden," Libby says after a while. "I've collected some of it."

Like ashes, Anke thinks. *Toss ashes into the garden and watch how flowers grow.*

"We had too many tiles. Enough to do both bathroom floors," Anke says haltingly. "After Ruth died, I smashed the rest and scattered them here. I cleaned out the shed and refused to let others go near it." She takes another deep breath. "But I'm glad someone's growing flowers in there again."

"I think Ruth is a lovely name," Libby says softly. She opens the door to the shed. Reaches for Anke's hand. As they step inside, she points to a row of young plants, still in their pots, their green berries shedding the last of their umbilical blooms. "Look, Anke. My tomatoes are growing."

Anke can almost taste them. Their soft flesh and gel-enveloped seeds.

Sunlight + Coloured Glass

- JOE WIEBE -

Danny points his bike down John and Sara's street. He's a little winded from the long climb up Cambie, but feeling good. His old bike still fits him like a glove, but the chain needs to be oiled — the squeak is embarrassing.

The houses on their street are all '50s bungalows with small yards and no driveways. He's been over to John and Sara's new house only once since they moved in three months earlier. Their housewarming. It was a pretty good party, though Danny struck out with the cute blonde co-worker of Sara's when he asked her to continue the night elsewhere.

He glides right up to their porch. The railing bends a little under the weight of his bike, and Danny makes a mental note to fix it even if it isn't part of the work they want him to do. John's call yesterday came out of the blue, the first time they'd talked since the party. He asked if Danny could do a couple days' work around the house, mainly some painting, and said they'd pay him $500 under the table. Though it sounded like too much money for only two days' work, Danny didn't hesitate. He certainly could use the cash.

John is on the phone when he opens the door. He gives Danny a quick smile and motions him into the cool interior of the house. Danny tunes out the phone conversation and looks around. He stops in the entrance to the living room. Morning sunlight streams through a row of antique leaded glass squares bordering the top of the big bay window, sending dappled shafts of orange and pink dust motes across the room. If Danny had his camera, he would definitely shoot that light, but the XL-1 is in hock along with the rest of his film equipment, and even the promised five hundred would only go halfway to getting it back.

He is still staring at the beams of light when John calls from a few rooms away. "Dan? Where'd you go?"

The scene playing out in Danny's mind dissolves back into the empty living room, but a kernel of an idea for a film doesn't disappear. He takes one last look at the light before following John's voice.

They meet in the marble and stainless steel kitchen under a chain lattice of copper-bottom pots strung from the ceiling. Danny pulls John's handshake into a hug. He waits for his old friend's stiffness to soften until the embrace grows uncomfortably long.

"Hey, buddy. It's good to see you," he says.

John smiles back at him. "Yeah, you too. How you been keeping?"

"Can't complain. Little of this, little of that, you know."

"Don't I, though. Summer's treating you well?"

"Sure," Danny replies easily, not thinking about the bills, the creditors, the waiting and wondering. "Can't you tell from my tan?"

John stretches out a pasty white arm. "You'd think all the radiation from my monitor would give me a little colour at least."

"Just cancer, dude. And haemorrhoids." Stupid, he thinks. What a stupid thing to say.

John chuckles. "Coffee?"

"Sure." Danny eyes the fancy Italian espresso maker on the counter, but John pours from a stainless steel thermos into a matching mug.

"Black, right?"

John is dressed up, at least in Danny's eyes: dark pants that appear silky in the bright halogen, gelled hair, a pressed shirt and chunky black leather shoes. Danny feels grungy in his shorts, T-shirt and scuffed sneakers.

"I have a meeting downtown in about an hour," John says. "I should probably show you what we want done."

"Sure thing, John-boy. Point me at the paintbrushes."

The main job is to strip and re-paint the six-foot wooden fence that encloses the yard. The boards are still in good shape, but the old brown paint is peeling off in big patches. The new paint is green, darker than the lawn, but lighter than the fir tree that leans over the house.

"I figure a day for the stripping and another for the painting." John speaks as they walk along the fence. "And we want the window frames in the same colour, too."

The paint cans and some new brushes, a roller and scrapers sit in a tidy pile in a little prefab shed in a corner of the backyard. Along with two pristine mountain bikes, some gardening tools, a stepladder and a neatly coiled hose. Everything is too clean. If this were a location shoot, Danny would ask the set dressers to dirty it up a bit.

He starts stripping the old paint as soon as John goes back inside the house. The day is warm, so he has his shirt off in no time. The work is easy, and he finds himself remembering the summer after their first year at the University of British Columbia when he and John worked for College Pro Painters. Those were the days. Long hours, parties almost every night. At the end of the summer, there was less money for school than he'd expected, but at least he had some great memories.

The déjà vu of the moment is strong, but there's no Nirvana

cranked on the ghetto blaster and no skinny little John-boy with his glasses and pale skin. Danny's belly hangs over his belt a little now, too. That certainly is different.

He's about a quarter of the way around the yard when John comes out to tell him he's off to his meeting. He hands Danny a set of house keys.

"Feel free to grab a drink, or make yourself a sandwich or whatever. I won't be back 'til late in the afternoon." John examines Danny's work. "Lookin' good, Dan."

Danny lasts about twenty minutes longer. He goes to the bathroom even though he doesn't really have to. He doesn't look through the medicine cabinet — he already did that at the housewarming party and didn't find anything interesting. He walks through the house, looking in each silent room. He touches the duvet on their bed, tests the smooth, sliding mechanism of their dresser drawers, caresses the cool slickness of some of Sara's lingerie. She doesn't have anything particularly risqué, but he likes the feel of her black silk negligée between his fingers.

In a hallway, there is a framed photo of John and Sara on a tropical beach. Thailand, Danny remembers. At the housewarming party, they talked about how they wished they could move there. And their other friends, all those couples — the guys with identical haircuts, the women with trim, yoga-toned bodies and bright, unwrinkled eyes who nursed a glass of white wine for hours — they laughed with John and Sara over the joke. Yeah right, move to Thailand, what a crazy idea. Any of those couples could afford to do it, Danny thinks. If they wanted to, they could do it. He almost said something at the party, but by the time he thought of a witty remark, the conversation had moved on.

Danny shakes his head, still staring at the photo. Back in their university days, he would never have imagined John and Sara getting together. They were a tight trio in those days, and Danny was the glue. Sara had a thing for him — he knew by the way she hung on his every word — but he saw her as a buddy. And John was his sidekick, following Danny's lead in everything.

He was surprised when John and Sara began dating shortly

after graduation. And their wedding only a year after that. Danny was the best man, though they hadn't seen each other much since school. But it made sense since he had brought them together in a way. He remembered little of the ceremony or reception, in part because of how drunk he got, but also because he was exhausted. He'd spent the year after graduation putting together the funding and crew to shoot a twenty-five-minute short that he wrote and directed. It was a harrowing ride of triumphs and failures that culminated in a sloppy film — he could admit that now — that was rejected by all the festivals. It also sent him into personal bankruptcy, a hole he was still trying to climb out of.

Danny didn't see much of John and Sara over the first few years after their wedding, but that was only the natural drift that happens to university friends as they start their real lives. Eventually, their paths began to cross again, and they developed a comfortable routine after a while. John and Sara would invite him over for dinner at their apartment every few months.

In the kitchen, he considers cracking a beer, but there are only three in the fridge, so it'd be pretty obvious. He grabs a Coke instead and stretches out on a lounge chair on the cedar deck. When he wakes up, his watch reads 2:37. Power nap or what, he thinks as he gets back to work, expecting John home at any time.

Danny is about two-thirds finished with the stripping when he hears the patio door slide open. He turns to say something witty about John being late, but stops. It's Sara.

"Hey, Dan," she says, stepping carefully down off the deck in pointy shoes. Even with the heels, she is well short of his own six feet. He likes taller women, but she's pretty. She keeps herself slim and doesn't hide what curves she has. Her reddish-brown hair is pulled back in a pony-tail. Tan pants and a white fitted shirt with the top two buttons undone. Make-up. Her job is pretty high up in the university administration, so she has to dress up.

Lifting his eyes back up to her face, he says, "Hey Sara, lookin' gorgeous as usual."

She smiles back at him and stops a few feet away. Too far for a hug.

"It's roasting today," she says, her nose crinkling as if she smells something funny. Danny has always liked that crinkle and the cute spray of freckles, too. "I hope you're wearing sunscreen."

He likes the idea of Sara looking at his body and sucks his gut in.

"Nah, I'm pretty well impervious by now." The back of his neck does feel a little warm. Tomorrow, he'll wear a ball cap.

"Looks like you've been working hard," she says without even glancing at the fence. "You about ready to call it quits for the day?"

"Another half an hour." He wants to get at least to the big fir so John won't think he's been slacking off.

"OK, you workhorse. But you're staying for dinner, right? I told Jonathan to buy steaks."

"Sounds great." His mouth waters at the thought.

He watches Sara as she walks back to the house, lets his eyes slide over her tight little ass. She glances back as she goes through the patio doors, and he waves the scraper.

He is almost even with the tree when John calls to him from the patio. "Quitting time, Dan-o. Come up here and grab yourself a beer."

Danny hears the reassuring sound of ice bouncing into a cooler. When he steps up onto the deck, John hands him an open Heineken.

"Cheers." They clink bottles and Danny slugs back half the beer.

"So good after a day in the sun," he says, and tilts back the green bottle again.

"It's good after a day dealing with hard-ass clients, too, let me tell you." John sips his beer. He has changed into baggy shorts and a loud Hawaiian shirt. Danny can't help but smile at his prissy brown leather sandals.

John waves him towards the cooler where, to Danny's relief, there are another dozen bottles among the ice cubes. Danny pops the top off another with the opener on his key chain and sits down across from his friend, who is staring at the fence with a distant look on his face. Before Danny can think of an excuse for why he hasn't finished the stripping, John smiles at him.

"This is great."

"Yeah, it's coming along." Danny nods at the fence.

"No, I mean, it's great to drink beers with you on a summer evening. Like the good old days." He reaches over to clink bottles again.

"Damn straight." Danny stops himself from chugging the rest of his second beer. He'll try to time it so that he finishes it when John finishes his first.

The patio door swishes open and Sara comes through with a platter of raw steaks slathered in spices.

"Now, don't you men worry about getting up to help or anything. I'm sure I can manage on my own." She's changed out of her work clothes into a sleeveless summer dress. Her hair, loose now, brushes the freckled tops of her shoulders. Danny likes the bulge of her little biceps as she carries the platter.

"Like she'd ever let me close to the barbecue." John winks.

"You're on salad duty, buster, in about twenty minutes." As she leans over to kiss John, Danny glimpses white lace and freckled skin down the drooping neck of her dress. When he looks back up, he finds her eyes on his.

"Anything I can do?" he asks. "Set the table?"

"No. You worked hard all day. Just relax."

As Sara bustles in and out of the house, John tells Danny about some clients who are complaining about a Flash Sequence on their website. Danny tries not to let his eyes glaze over. He forces John to finish his beer by fetching him another without asking.

The slight buzz from Danny's third beer competes with the growing warmth of his sunburned neck. And neither helps him focus on John's story. Luckily, Sara interrupts with, "Salad time, Jonathan."

She stays at the barbecue while John goes inside. She flips a sizzling steak, tests it with a finger, licks the juice off her fingertip.

"Smells great," Danny says, going over to stand beside her.

"How do you want yours done?"

"Medium rare if you can."

"Sure, no problem." She squints up at his face, the sun behind him. "Can I have a sip of your beer?"

He hands her the bottle and she takes a little swig, then another, then hands it back. She tests the biggest steak again.

"Jonathan likes his burnt." Her nose crinkles again. "But I like a little blood on my plate."

Danny has trouble reconciling this confident meat-eater with the quiet, pale vegetarian Sara was back in university. He likes her better now, and he wonders when she changed.

They eat on the deck. Danny savours each bite of his steak, sopping up the juice on his plate with a piece of salty focaccia. John opens a bottle of thick, purple Argentine Shiraz. Danny loves red wine, but rarely can afford anything this good; he wants to hold it in his mouth and never swallow.

After dinner, Danny helps clean up the dishes, and then they all return outside to sit in the waning sunlight. He turns down their offer of coffee, content with ice-cold Heinekens.

An hour or two later, Sara is telling them about a member of her staff who complains about everything — the office is either too hot or too cold, his chair isn't ergonomic, the computer screens emit radiation. Danny smiles as her face grows red, fired by indignation. This is the Sara he remembers from their university days, but back then the things that pissed her off were homelessness and the lack of support for prostitutes.

It's close to midnight by the time Danny finds nothing but icy water in the cooler. How many has he had? He spots four or five empties beside his chair, knows he put at least as many in the box beside the cooler. He looks around. Just John. When did Sara go inside? John has a sweater on now. Danny shivers. All he has is the T-shirt he put back on when they ate.

"Man, I'm bagged," he says. His head is thick, and he yawns uncontrollably. No doubt Sara is making up a bed for him. Clean sheets and a real mattress, nicer than his flat old futon.

"Guess we better call it a night, eh?"

When Danny comes out of the bathroom, John is standing by the front door.

"I don't want you weaving home on your bike so I called you a cab, OK?"

John tells the taxi driver Danny's address, which pisses him off, like he doesn't know his own address, but he decides not to make a deal of it.

"Thanks for dinner," Danny says. "Say good night to Sara."

"I will. Good night, Dan." John hands the driver a twenty-dollar bill, and with a tap on the roof, sends the cab on its way.

Danny doesn't arrive until just before noon the next day, so he goes straight to the backyard without checking to see if John is inside. His bike is in the shed. He should have put it in the trunk of the taxi the night before. It would have saved him the hassle of three buses this morning.

As he works, he thinks about the film idea that came to him in the living room yesterday. He's surprised at how much it's grown in his mind. It's almost all there, start to finish: a conventional, well-off young couple, seemingly perfect — except for a dark secret.

He is a few slats away from the sidewalk when a black Jetta pulls up. John gets out of the car and walks over.

"Hey, Dan-o. How's the head? I was hangin' a bit myself this morning, and I know you had a few more than I did."

"It's all good," Danny says. "That half-a-cow I ate soaked up all the booze, I think."

"Yeah, those steaks were good," John agrees. "Hey, I have some clients coming over for a meeting in about an hour, so let me know before then if you need anything."

Danny wants to talk to John about the film idea. He knows John will get jazzed on it, and maybe he'd agree to loan Danny the money to get his camera back from the pawn shop. Hell, Danny could give him Producer credit. But the main thing is the house. He needs to use John and Sara's house. It's perfect for the film.

"Do you have time for lunch, like a sandwich or something?" Danny asks. His stomach is actually a little upset — probably not used to the steak — but this way they could talk.

"I just ate downtown, but you go right ahead." John pauses on his way into the house. "And don't worry if you can't finish before Sara and I leave tonight."

They're leaving? A glimmer from last night's conversation refuses to drop into focus.

"Our time-share in Kelowna, remember? We're leaving as soon as Sara gets home."

"Right," Danny says. "Right."

"You can take all weekend if you like. We won't be back 'til Monday some time." John disappears inside the house.

Danny stares at the closed door for a moment before returning to the fence.

When John's clients arrive, Danny is in the stifling hot shed, opening the first paint can. He hears them talking in the front yard, then — "Jonathan! How are you?"

Danny starts in the corner of the yard where he can see into John's office. While he paints, he surreptitiously watches John talking to his clients. Danny can't hear anything through the closed window, but from the smiles and laughter, he can tell they like John. But John seems fake, acting or something. It's too bad, Danny thinks. He's glad he never has to do that.

Later, after he hears the clients leave, Danny waits for the sound of the patio door, imagines John holding out a couple cold beers, beckoning him to take a break. Danny will tell him about the film and John will offer him some cash.

After a few minutes, Danny stops painting and looks toward the house, but the door remains closed. He stares at the dark mirrored surfaces of the window-panes. There's a reflection there: the backyard, the half-painted fence, and a figure — himself, paintbrush in hand. He closes his eyes for a moment, and then turns back to the fence.

A few hours later, Sara comes out to the edge of the deck. He turns when she calls his name, but stays by the fence.

"I hope you won't have to work all weekend," she says, holding up one hand to shade her eyes from the bright sun. Her yoga pants are the colour of the lawn, and her sleeveless top is sky blue.

"Nah, I've only got a couple more hours left."

"Good. Well, we'll bring you back some wine, if we don't drink it all."

Now he remembers — they're spending the weekend touring wineries.

John steps out of the house behind her. "We better hit the road, Sar. I want to get over the Coquihalla before dark."

"Did you remember to pay the man for his hard work?"

"Oh, shit! I forgot to stop at the bank machine." John looks at Sara for help, but she just frowns back at him, so he turns back to Danny. "I can write a cheque, though. That's cool, right Dan?"

It isn't cool. With Danny's bad credit, the cheque will take a couple of weeks to clear.

"Jonathan, under the table means cash," Sara says. "I think I've got a hundred or so. How much do you have?"

They pool their paper money and come up with $240, which John hands to him. "I'll get the rest to you on Monday, OK? Sorry, buddy."

Danny pockets the cash and wishes them a great weekend.

When Danny hears them drive off, he puts the paintbrush down and stretches his back. He's done for the night. He won't be able to finish before dark anyway. After putting everything away, he goes inside and washes up in the bathroom. He manages to get most of the paint splatters off his hands, but he still smells like paint, sunscreen and sweat.

He shrugs at himself in the mirror and removes his clothes. Their shower is a little room blocked off from the rest of the bathroom by a wall of glass. The tiles are cool and rough under his feet. The jets of water feel good on his sore shoulders — the pressure is stronger than his shower at home. He smells the contents of each bottle and settles on two that must be Sara's — minty shampoo and lavender conditioner. He pours apricot shower gel over a coarse loofah and scrubs his skin raw. When he turns off the water, he feels pink and new, cleaner than he has been in years.

John's clothes are way too small for him, so Danny is stuck with what he's been wearing in the hot sun all day. He delays dressing, though, and looks through the medicine cabinet. Same as at the party, nothing interesting or worth trying, no pill bottles with strange names. But what's this? Something new after all — a home pregnancy test. Unopened. What does that mean? That they're trying to get pregnant, but Sara hasn't missed her period yet? Or maybe she had a scare, but is too chicken to check. Danny returns it to the shelf and closes the cabinet. He smiles at his reflection. The possibility of a pregnancy is the perfect addition to his screenplay.

He's tempted to shave, but likes the look of the stubble on his face. He uses some styling gel to make his hair look purposely dishevelled. Eventually, he gets dressed. Reluctantly.

He checks the fridge. No beer. He pours himself a tumbler full of vodka from the bottle he finds in the freezer and carries the glass and bottle into the living room. He eyes the big flat-screen TV — they probably have a hundred channels — but no, he should think about his film. He doesn't like working on paper; he prefers mapping it out in his head first. He stretches out on the leather sofa, props his head on the arm, and gets to work.

A thump on the door wakes Danny early the next morning. Where is he? He sees the empty vodka bottle, and finds the time on the VCR — 6:17. He can't remember the last time he was up this early. His head is surprisingly clear, but then again, he probably crashed long before midnight.

He remembers the noise and checks the door. The Saturday *Globe and Mail.* He picks it up and carries it back into the living room, but stops in the hallway. Warm shafts of sunlight, filtered through the stained glass, shoot across the room. They're even more spectacular than the morning when he first saw them. He tosses the paper aside and drops into a crouch, finding the perfect camera angle from the bottom right corner of the doorway. He stays down on his haunches, working out the scenes where he would use the light, until his knees start to ache. Then, he goes outside to finish the work.

The fence takes him the rest of the morning, and then he starts on the window frames. As he works, he lets ideas for the film roll around in his head. Characters come and go; scenes are shot and then discarded. Bit by bit, he smoothes the rough edges of the idea.

Late in the afternoon, Danny is painting the frame around the big living room window when he realizes it's the last one. He'll be done in ten minutes, which is good because he's tired. He has pushed himself hard all day.

He twists his body to stretch his aching back. His perch on the ladder gives him a clear view of the street. It would be a good opening shot for the film. Houses similar to this one, their yards clearly marked by a fence or a hedge, SUVs and Volvos parked in front, here or there a sportier Audi or BMW. A rusty old pickup truck beside a yard where a young man mows the lawn. Even as Danny watches, the mower's motor dies, and the young man pushes it over to the truck. He empties the bag and lifts the mower over the tailgate. As he drives past John and Sara's house a minute later, he lifts a lazy hand, but Danny, up on the ladder, doesn't notice. The perfect climax for his film is playing out in his mind. The landscaper will reveal the dark secret and shatter the yuppie couple's perfect life. Danny is ready. When he gets home, he'll start writing. He has it all now.

As he turns back to the window, his balance on the ladder shifts slightly. He reaches out to steady himself. His fingertips catch the window frame, but the brush handle taps the pane lightly. Steady again, he pulls his hand away. There is a crack. He stares at it in disbelief. He hardly touched the glass. He blinks his eyes, but the crack is still there, splitting one of the small panels of leaded glass almost perfectly in half.

Danny feels sick, like when he was a kid and he did something he knew he'd get in trouble for. His stomach churns. He swallows. He puts the brush down, and carefully touches the fractured pane of amber glass. It still feels solid. Why did it crack so easily?

Danny closes his eyes. He tries to think of scenes from the film, but all he can see is the cracked glass. John and Sara should be able to replace it; they can take the money out of his pay.

But even as he tries to calm himself, his hand curls into a fist. He feels his bicep flex and his fist punch through the cracked pane. He opens his eyes wide to see the empty frame, only slightly larger than his fist. Two neat halves of leaded glass rest on the living room carpet inside. He moves his fist to the next pane of coloured glass and punches. This one shatters into several pieces, one sharp enough to draw a little blood. He punches the next one, and the one after that, until he has broken all the panes of coloured glass along the top of the living room window.

It takes him about five minutes to finish painting the window frame. He carries the ladder to the shed and cleans up the paint cans and brushes. He walks his bike out to the front yard, locks the house and drops the keys John gave him into the mailbox.

Danny pedals hard down the big hill on Cambie, fast enough to keep up with the cars, fast enough that the wind pulls tears from the corners of his eyes.

Katja

- LOUISE BERGEN PRICE -

Irkutzk, Siberia. March 13, 1956.

Katja was afraid to open the letter, the first since she and her daughters had been exiled here eleven years ago. Hope had let her down before. Her breath caught in her lungs, and her body ached.

"Sascha," she said to her four-year-old grandchild, "please fetch me a cup of water."

Sascha filled the cup from the water bucket by the door and inched toward her, biting his lower lip. Although Katja took the full cup in both hands, water spilled on the table and darkened the edge of the envelope lying there. She pushed it aside.

"Oma." Sascha tugged at her sleeve. "Will you read your letter?"

"Later," Katja said. She pulled him onto her lap; he snuggled closer, sighed and fell asleep. Katja rested her chin on Sascha's head. The letter with the stamp from Canada lay just out of reach. Liese would be home soon; they would read it together.

Thüringen Refugee Camp. August 1945.

Katja heard her daughter's footsteps well before she burst into their compartment. "Mam, we have to leave. We won't be safe much longer. Germany is going to be divided among the Allies and all refugees sent back to their place of birth. We've got to leave!"

Katja paled. "But we're German citizens now!"

"Doesn't matter. We were born in the Soviet Union. Come on, let's get ready."

She grabbed her mother's arm and tugged as if they could go now, this minute.

"No, Liese. Wait . . ."

"I'm telling you we don't have time! Start packing. I'll get the girls and we'll leave tonight with the others. They say the British zone is safer. We can apply to emigrate from there."

"No!" Katja hadn't meant to scream, only to get Liese's attention, but the hum and chatter in the surrounding compartments stopped. Katja's hand trembled on her daughter's shoulder. "We'll go, Liese. As soon as your brothers get here."

"Mam! You don't understand! We've waited for weeks; we can't wait longer. What do you think will happen to us when the Russian soldiers get here?" She pulled away so abruptly that Katja's hand dropped. "Oh, what's the use?"

"Liese, wait . . ."

But Liese pushed aside the curtain. The barrack door slammed.

Katja pressed her forehead against the windowpane. Dear God, if only the boys would arrive. Why didn't they come? Heina and Jasch had been conscripted during the German occupation of Neustadt, their Mennonite village in Ukraine. When the Germans retreated in 1943, Katja and her remaining five children had joined the trek of refugees fleeing westward with the German army. They travelled by wagon, foot and train through western Ukraine, Poland and into Germany, finally arriving at this refugee camp in Thüringen. Two years later, sixteen-year-old Peter was conscripted. He was so young. So lost in his uniform, like thousands of others sent to fight Hitler's last battles.

Now, soldiers were returning to their families. Heina, Jasch and Peter would too. Any day now. She'd kept their clothes for when they'd escape together. To Canada. Freedom.

Dear God in Heaven, let them come soon. Liese was right. They had only a few days. But she'd deserted her children once before — how could she leave without them now?

Neustadt, Ukraine. July 1931.

Katja knew everyone in this village, but today there were no friendly greetings. Her husband, Heinrich, had just been arrested and jailed for not paying taxes levied three times in as many months, their house, barn and possessions sold, and Katja put out on the street with their children: Anna, three months old; Heina, only ten; Peter, Susie, Liese and Jasch in-between. A few people mumbled something like "Good day" and hurried on. Was it pity she saw in their eyes, or fear for their own safety?

"Hey, *kulaks*! How does it feel to be poor?" A group of young boys in ragged shirts and dirt-stained pants ran alongside.

Heina's fists clenched.

"Heina! Keep walking. We're almost at Tante Tina's. See? There it is."

The small room Tina's husband cleaned out for them was dim and smelled of cows. An old wooden table and two chairs stood near the window; straw filled a back corner.

Katja lay awake into the night while Anna fussed and drank, the tiny mouth tugging a small comfort at Katja's breast. Only last week Katja had handed out cooked potatoes to beggars; now she and her children would join the crowds that streamed from door to door.

Within days, the older children knew what to do, returning with sugar beets, pumpkins, potato peelings, sunflower seeds. Seldom bread — the Soviet government's Red Broom Brigade had swept every grain from attics and storehouses. Soon Heina, Susie, Liese and Jasch resembled the skinny urchins who had taunted them. Peter whined and chewed on anything he found. Anna barely woke to drink.

The old woman has kind eyes. Her gnarled fingers gently shift Katja's shawl to touch Anna's cheek.

She turns to Katja. "Feed the boy."

"What?"

"This one will not live — but that one may." She nods at Peter. "Let him drink."

"Get out!"

"She's getting weak; she'll hardly notice."

"Out. OUT!" Katja screams.

"Mam? What's wrong?" Liese knelt beside her.

"A bad dream, Liese. I'm all right. Go back to sleep."

Katja propped herself up on her elbow. Peter whimpered; she rubbed the nape of his neck until she felt him relax. She fell asleep.

The black cat silhouetted against the early morning sky has a kitten dangling from her mouth.

What will the mother eat? Mice, rabbits, squirrels — they're all soup now. She will show it mercy.

The kitten thrashes in the water, claws raking the metal bucket. Katja looks away, presses fingers on ears, and waits. Then she carries the bucket to the manure pile. But the emptied bucket is heavy, scrabbling with mewing kittens. All Katja thinks of is soup. Rich and meaty, with chunks of potato, carrot and onion, and lots of fresh dill.

NO! Katja hurls the bucket, but instead of kittens, babies tumble out, twig-like limbs tangled in dill-weed; faces just like Anna's. Katja opens her mouth, but no scream sounds.

"Mama! I have to pee." Peter wriggled against her. "Mama! Take me outside." Katja sat up, confused. Beside her, Anna slept peacefully. She put her face to the baby's till she felt Anna's breath.

"Mama!"

"Yes, Peter. Let's go."

Heina brought home a head of cabbage that day. He did not say from whom or where, and Katja didn't ask. She chewed a mouthful until it was soft, scooped a bit onto her finger and slid it onto Anna's tongue. Anna turned her head, and the cabbage dribbled out of her mouth.

Katja withheld her news until after dark and the children lay in a row on the straw. "I'm going away tomorrow," she said. "If Anna doesn't get milk soon, she'll die. I'm taking her and Peter to Oma and Opa's in Sagradovka. They still have a cow. And a big garden."

"Take us too!"

"I wish I could, but I was barely able to borrow enough money as it is. I'll be back. Three or four days at the most."

Silence. Then Jasch's small voice. "Mam? Can you bring us a bread?"

"I'll bring a big loaf, Jasch. I promise. And you listen to Heina and take care of each other while I'm gone."

"Yes, Mam."

She left early in the morning, when the children were still drowsy with sleep, and arrived in Sagradovka the next day, exhausted and sick. Three weeks later, she was finally strong enough to return home.

As the train crept from village to village, Katja sat straight, eyes ever watchful. Under her shawl she clutched a loaf of heavy rye, enough to keep her older children alive for a week. *If* they had survived — she'd had no news.

Along the tracks lay scattered bundles of rags. Beggars. Some were alive. A boy Jasch's age looked up as the train rumbled by, his face all eyes and sharp bones. Others lay dead where they'd fallen, children and old people mostly. Who would show them mercy and cover them with earth?

The stench of decay seeped into the train where passengers jostled on wooden benches and crowded the aisles. No one spoke — a wrong word could mean prison or death. They stared at windows, at their own feet, anywhere but at their own terror mirrored in another's eyes.

The train groaned to a halt. Katja stumbled onto the platform. "Christ have mercy . . . have mercy . . . Christ . . ."

She averted her eyes as she passed the beggars.

She saw Jasch first. He was trudging down the dusty road, dragging a sack behind him. So. At least one was safe.

"Jasch," she shouted, her hoarse voice strained. "Jasch." He turned and ran, hurling himself at her, his small body solid and real.

"Can we go home now, Mam? I don't want to beg anymore."

"Yes, Jasch. Yes." Katja wiped her eyes on her sleeve. "Where are the others?"

"Begging. Except for Liese. She stayed home."

Katja walked faster.

"Mam!" Jasch tugged at her hand. "Wait, wait!"

She stopped, bent to hug him. "Oh, Jasch. You don't know how happy I am."

Liese dropped the bucket of water she was carrying toward the house and ran as she shouted, "Heina! Susie! Come quick. Mam's home!"

They swarmed her, fought for her hands, tugged at her clothes. "You're back, Mam." "Where were you so long? We thought maybe you were dead." "Where are Anna and Peter?"

Their shoulder blades were sharp under her fingers. She cupped each face in her hands, kissed cheeks, eyebrows, foreheads. "Anna and Peter are fine," she said. "Oma's taking good care of them. I got sick on the train, really sick, and I wasn't strong enough to come back sooner. But you . . . I can hardly believe you're all well! What did you eat?"

"Corn. Liese cooks it for us on Tante Tina's stove. And we begged . . ."

"Mam?" Jasch pulled at her skirt. "Mam, I'm hungry. Can I have some bread?"

"Of course, Jasch. Let's eat."

Later that evening, while the others slept, Heina pulled her toward the sack that lay propped in the corner. It was half-filled with yellow cornmeal. Katja cupped her hands and let the coarse meal trickle through her fingers.

"Where did you get this?"

"The cornfield," he answered. "I snuck out late at night . . ."

"Oh, Heina. You could have been whipped. Shot, even!"

"No, no, Mam. Look. I used Papa's old coat." He turned it inside out, showed her the lining attached to the bottom hem. "I made holes in the pockets, and I stuffed the corn down into the lining. No one could see.

"I told the children that someone brought us the corn at night, which had to be kept secret. We husked the corn every morning, plucked the kernels, and dried them in the sun. When the sack was half full, I took it to the mill — Onkel Wiebe didn't ask any questions." Heina stopped. "Why are you crying, Mam? Are you angry?"

She shook her head. "No, Heina." She pulled him close; Heina hugged her back.

That night she lay very still, listening to her sleeping children. The straw rustled each time one of them stirred. Katja's face was wet, her fear and dread washed away to release an overwhelming joy.

She owed her children. She had deserted them when they needed her.

Thüringen Refugee Camp. August 1945.

Dust layered the barrack window through which Katja watched her daughters in the meadow between the buildings. Anna sat cross-legged, laughing. She held a daisy in her hands and plucked its petals, one by one.

Susie plucked at a daisy too. *He loves me, he loves me not, he loves me . . .* Eleven-year-old Tina lay on her back, hands behind her head, and eyes on the clouds. Tina, more than the others, was a child of these times. She did not remember her father; she'd been born in 1934, a year after he was released from prison, and she was only four when he was arrested the second and final time.

Liese joined her sisters, shoulders hunched, hands deep in her pockets. She said something, and both girls dropped their daisies. Tina sat up, and all four turned toward the barrack window.

Katja pulled on a sweater and tied her scarf under her chin. As she walked down the makeshift corridor, she heard murmured voices and the clatter of dishes. Trunks and suitcases scraped the floor: Liese was right; everyone had heard the news.

She hurried to the railway station where, hours later, Anna and Tina found her.

"Come, Mam. It's time for supper."

She stared at them.

"Mam? Come." They took her hands and led her back to the camp.

She returned to the station each morning to scan the bulletin boards, search the faces of young men stepping off the trains, and to ask, "Do you know the Penner boys? Heina, Jasch and Peter from Neustadt?"

Some ignored her; others shook their heads.

Today, she told herself each morning. *If they don't arrive today, we're leaving without them.*

Weeks later, when the Russians rolled into camp, she was still waiting. They and the other remaining families were given a few hours to gather provisions and to pack before being loaded onto transport trucks and taken to the railway station.

"Why so gloomy?" a young soldier asked. "You're going home, aren't you?"

"We have no home," Katja answered.

Katja and her daughters climbed on board. The boxcar had rough wooden bunks along each side, but all were taken. They spread one blanket on the floor, covered themselves with another and huddled together. Liese sat beside them, her face cold and eyes distant.

The doors squealed shut, and the train jerked forward. One day slid into another as the train rumbled eastward, through trench-scarred fields and ruined cities where children and old women combed the rubble. Charred tanks and trucks lay mired in shadowed ruts and ditches. Farther and farther east, through the mountains, and then the familiar steppes of Ukraine.

But the train moved on. They were no longer refugees returning home, but prisoners headed for Siberian slave camps. The soldiers and guards treated them with contempt, unafraid to use their whips and guns.

Once each day the train ground to a stop. As the doors screeched open, the guards shoved in their food ration: a piece of stale bread, occasionally accompanied by a slice of salt fish. Never enough fresh water.

If the guards permitted, the weary passengers scrambled out, breathing in large gulps of fresh air before searching out bushes or grass clumps. After the first few days, they simply squatted in the open fields. Anything was more private than a bucket on the floor of a closed train car.

Days became weeks, and the train moved on, east and north. At times it hurtled across the steppe; sometimes it sat on a side-track for hours or days, waiting for engine repairs or a freight train that eventually rushed by.

Everyone, especially children and old people, suffered from lice, dysentery and starvation. One day, a baby died. Hour after hour the mother sat, rocking her dead child and crooning. Katja tried to take the child, but the young mother clutched the ragged bundle tighter. It was Liese, still sullen and angry, who finally succeeded. She wrapped her arms around mother and child and rocked them both. As she rocked, she sang, *"Weil ich Jesu Schäflein bin . . ."* The mother quieted and fell asleep on Liese's shoulder. Liese took the baby into her arms.

Katja is a child again. Her hand in her father's, she skips at his side, their arms swinging apart, then together. They are going to the pasture to check the newborn lambs. "Papa, I learned a Psalm in school today. Want to hear it?" And before he can reply, she chants, "The Lord is my shepherd, I shall not want."

An early morning rain has left sparkles on the green field. White lambs amid yellow dandelions. Blue sky.

Katja picks a dandelion, then another and another. "Papa, look. Sunshine!" she calls. The trickle of juices streaks her arms black.

"Katja," her mother chides, "be more careful."

In the pasture, a ewe lies panting, too exhausted to clean its new-born shiny with blood and mucous. Papa wraps the lamb in a towel and rubs it dry.

"I am Jesus' little lamb," Katja sings.

A dark wall rises from the ground; a blinding light roars through the blackness and tears her hand from her father's.

She is one with the darkness. Sheep race from one side of the railway car to the other, sharp hooves trampling the lambs at their feet. Blood pools, then spreads in a film. The floor is slippery.

The Lord is my shepherd . . .

Papa! Take me home!

"Let me die!" someone screamed. "I want to die!" It was Neta Braun's eighty-year-old grandmother.

"I'm coming, Oma. Coming." Neta steered the old woman over and around sleeping bodies towards the bucket.

Katja buried her face in her sleeve against the foetid smell and drifted off again.

When she awoke, light streamed through the window onto the young mother curled on the floor, her head in Liese's lap.

Katja reached for the baby. Liese stirred. "Here, Mam," she said, "we'll use my shawl."

The young mother sat up drowsily and watched. She reached out and laid her thin fingers against her baby's waxen face. "She's with Jesus now," she said.

"Yes," Katja said. "With Jesus."

That night, when the train stopped, they scraped a shallow grave beside the tracks. Two days later, they dug a grave for the mother.

As the train moved north, the steppe gave way to marshland and bog, then lakes and forests. When they stopped, the air was chill. One evening, as they climbed into their boxcar, Anna pointed. "Mam. Look!"

It had been overcast all day; now the sun broke through the clouds. Among black spruce trees, larches blazed, lit by fire that did not consume.

Katja caught her breath.

"Hurry, Mam. We're going." Liese urged Katja forward into the gloom and stench of the car.

Throughout the night, fire burned behind Katja's eyelids, and a piercing voice commanded: *Take off your shoes, lead my children home. Yes, God, yes. We're going.*

Occasionally, the train rolled through a collection of barracks surrounded by row on row of coiled barbed wire. Sometimes they saw groups of prisoners shuffling along, shoulders bowed, legs shackled. Always, guards in warm coats and boots, gloved hands carrying rifles, bayonets fixed and ready. Once Katja saw a young man of nineteen or twenty, jacket too tight across his shoulders, pants ragged around his ankles.

"Jasch!" she cried out.

But the young man who turned toward them was not Jasch.

The train rolled on. Finally, after six weeks of travelling, they stopped at a small railway station and were ordered off the train. That night they slept in rough wooden barracks; the next day they were marched deep into the forest to small shacks that were to be their homes.

Light slanted through cracks between boards and filtered through holes in the sod roof. It was November and bitterly cold. A new life began. Mornings, they were marched through the dark, wading through waist-high snow to cut trees. After they lopped off and burned the branches, they lashed the logs together so teamsters with horses could pull them out. It was dark again when they stumbled back, weak with cold and hunger, for a meal of watery soup and a piece of wet rye bread. On the rare free day, Katja or one of the older girls plodded to the nearest village to barter clothing for bread or potatoes.

"Mam," Liese said one day in early spring as they gathered branches for firewood, "four more this week. The doctor says pneumonia, but everyone knows they starved."

"I know." Katja sat down on a log. *It's my fault,* she wanted to tell her daughter, but the words stuck in her throat.

"I talked to a driver yesterday." The log shifted as Liese sat down beside her. "There are other camps, where workers are treated much better. He says there's a good camp fifty kilometres away."

"But . . ."

"I'll go, Mam. If they let me stay, I'll send for the rest of you."

"But, Liese . . . how would you get there?"

"Walk."

"I'd hoped we could stay together . . ."

"And now we're starving in Siberia," Liese said. "I'm not ready to die. Not yet." She rose, added another branch to the bundle in her arms. "I'll leave on our next free day. By the time they notice, I'll be long gone. There are villages along the way — someone will take me in."

In the weeks after Liese left, Katja lived in constant fear. Fear of someone approaching her with news of Liese's death, that some team driver had found her body along the roadway. Or worse, that Liese had died alone in the cold. Somewhere.

And then the news came.

"Katherina Ivanovna?"

"Yes?"

The team driver tightened the knots that held his load of logs in place, then motioned to her. "Last week," he said, "such a nice spring day. I heard a bird sing. A little brown bird in a camp fifty kilometres away."

Katja closed her eyes for a moment. "The bird was safe and well?"

"Safe and well."

"Thank you."

Liese was safe and would send for them.

Irkutzk, Siberia. March 13, 1956.

"She's home, Oma! Mama's home." Sascha wriggled forward on Katja's lap and grabbed the letter. Waving it in the air, he ran to the door. "Mama, look! Oma says it's from Canada."

Liese sagged into a chair. "Why didn't you open it, Mam?"

"I thought we'd read it together."

"Eleven years in this god-forsaken wilderness, and now, a letter." Liese unfolded the paper. She stiffened. Muttered something Kajta couldn't hear.

"Liese! Who is it from? Read, read . . ."

Katja tugged the letter from her daughter's grasp. "Heina! My son! Dear God in Heaven, thank you. And listen, he's heard from Jasch. And Peter . . .

"Liese! Where are you going? Wait! Come back!"

An icy draft rattled the paper in Katja's hand and the door clicked shut.

Two Steps Forward

- ROXANNE WILLEMS SNOPEK -

At four-going-on-five, he's certainly able to sleep alone. Enough people have told me, and I know it's true, but in the dark I am unable to convince either one of us, and his fears are so real and my need to soothe him undeniable. During the night our bodies share space easily. His firm round rump blunts my sharp edges, and sometimes I can even feel his pulse, a rhythm familiar as a long-forgotten fragrance. The jarring confusion of our day vanishes in the softness of night, where there is no need for words.

When morning comes his damp head turns into my shoulder and his small hand reaches for my breast, and he disappears into silence again, leaving me far behind. At four-going-on-five, he's certainly able to sleep alone, but he doesn't want to. And neither do I. I recognize something in his clenched muscles, something that, when they ease into sleep, soothes me.

Before I dropped out, I read about a psychology experiment

conducted on baby monkeys. They were taken squealing from their mothers and put in bare wire cages, where their echoes bounced shrilly until the babies withdrew into the corners. On one side of each cage was a nipple, surrounded by nothing but cold metal; on the other side was a wire mother-substitute covered with a piece of soft cloth. The babies knew the milk came from the nipples, yet they clung to their wire "mothers" to the point of starvation, while white-coated scientists made notes on clipboards. What, I wondered at the time, was their earth-shattering conclusion? That baby monkeys would rather be comforted than fed? Who decided it was an either/or proposition? Even then, long before my son was born, I wondered at the stupidity of the human need for evidence. Then again, I merely imagined the viewpoint of the monkeys. The white-coats, I'm sure, would have chuckled and waved away my concern. No one likes to think himself cruel.

There is something about a silent child that stirs a great discomfort. When he sits with his plastic blocks, wordless but content, it's tolerable, and for a short time our demons fade away. But always they return, stalking, growling something only he can hear; then his eyes, swimming and dilated, will search out mine, and without a sound he'll creep into my lap, trembling, as if these uncertain arms could provide protection. I hold him and wonder, *What was it this time?* In my mind, I replay my words and actions of the day, the week, the month, but like a faulty videotape, all is fuzz and blur, revealing nothing.

It was during that endless, fleeting time between infancy and childhood that the burdens I'd thoughtlessly laid on him began to show. Words already late in coming trickled away, faded into silence before I'd had a chance to notice. I clutched at them in panic, refusing to open my eyes to my own accountability. Once, when I still sought a single answer and puzzled endlessly for a simple solution, I shook him. "WHY?" I screamed. "Why won't you tell me what's wrong? Why won't you talk?" He wet the bed that night. I haven't raised my voice since.

It was soon after, though, that I discovered what no one else knew, not even my own white-coats, the harried social workers.

Restless and riddled with guilt, I lay awake in the dark one night, wondering which of my many mistakes had scampered squirrel-like into my small son's brain, until a sound in the next room broke through my thoughts: a voice. I sat bolt upright, heart hammering, until I recognized it and realized . . . he was not completely silent. He still talked in his sleep. I found him tangled in the sheets, sprawled crossways in the narrow bed, blonde head twitching. "No. I can . . . Let me . . ." He argued stubbornly, as he once did with me.

I lowered myself shakily into a corner of his room, savouring the small sounds of my silent child speaking to someone in another world, scattering the threads of thought that must surely help me lead him back to this world. Of course, none of it made any sense to me.

But the next night I crept into his room after he had fallen asleep, hoping for another glimpse behind the veil of his mind. Minutes turned into hours. My legs went numb, my back began to ache, and I was dozing against the wall when the first small hiccuping sob jerked me awake. I crept awkwardly to the bed. His head moved restlessly against the pillow. "I thought . . . maybe," he mumbled. I leaned forward, certain that here would be the answers I craved. But the rest was lost. I didn't want to wake him and watch him shut me out again, but I couldn't leave. "It's okay. Mommy's here," I murmured, stroking his back lightly, afraid of what my touch might trigger. He shuddered a sigh, and I thought he'd slipped beneath the dream again, and I might as well go back to my own bed, when he said two words, two simple words, as distinct as anything he ever spoke in his short life.

"My Mommy."

Then he flopped over with satisfaction and sank promptly into a deep sleep. I stood motionless, stunned by gratitude and terror. I shifted him over, crawled under the covers, and pulled him close.

In my worst nightmares, I am still the woman I was when he entered my life, first unrecognized, then unwanted, then ignored. Timing, as they say, is everything and so it was that I bore a son. Perhaps I should have followed the advice so earnestly offered me at the time, to give him up. Perhaps it was already too late for him then. In this pain-stripped aftermath, there is no room for pretence, and so I confess it was nothing maternal that prompted my decision. Perverse, stubborn spite was the reason I chose to be my son's mother. I took him simply because he was mine. The white-coats allowed this, not out of wisdom, but from the dark knowledge that a toy fought over is often dropped and broken, or torn apart.

I wish his biggest fears were only nightmares. I wish I could say I loved him from the beginning. But my possessiveness had another source. He was my pawn, my ace, my own evidence. I had to prove my value, show them that I could do something right, that I, *I* could be a mother. That *even I* could do a better job than my parents had. I let his wide, clear gaze and smooth, soft toddler skin convince me to believe my own words. But I should have known that the body remembers everything.

"Gammy and Gammy," he cried, the last time I slammed their door. So small he was then — how could he possibly remember my rage? I haven't spoken to them since, but I still feel the sting of their words at odd moments. Nothing hurts as much as truth recognized by unready eyes. "Gammy and Gammy," he chanted at first, reminding me regularly of one more bridge burned in anger and panic. Gradually he stopped talking about them, and then he stopped talking altogether.

The experts that step in and out of the periphery of our lives watch us with eyes washed of hope, waiting to touch nail-holes before they'll believe the unbelievable. I still think something happened, some specific event that tipped the scales and made him retreat into the painted backdrop of his mind, but they tell me it's counter-productive to keep on asking "why?" Maybe for them, I think to myself. They have other cases nipping at their heels. But I'll keep asking why for the rest of my life, or until he answers me.

Although they don't expect me to understand — I can hear it in their flat voices — they tell me how my son's mind works, what he needs from me. They explain they have a name for that conviction held by young minds that everything revolves around them, is caused by them, or relates to them somehow. Egocentricity. A natural self-centredness.

I nod my head. Selfishness. This concept, at least, I understand. It's at the root of everything, isn't it? But this understanding is also the one thing that gives me hope. It's why I've decided to allow him to visit them again. Why I huddle on the freezing street, biting my lip as I watch my son disappear through his grandparents' doorway, hoping that perhaps this thin straw will be the one that pulls him out. It is why, for once, when I return for him, I will be the silent one. It's why, when the light fades and the shadows loom, I will clumsily share his small, narrow bed, throwing my poor flesh down as a peace offering to the demons.

I tell myself I'm not giving up; I'm growing up. Even on days when it seems we're taking two steps forward and three steps back, I remind myself that at least we're on the road now. We're going *somewhere*.

I stand there a moment longer, shrugging my too thin coat up against the biting wind. It'll be a long walk home, the snow-packed asphalt hard beneath my feet, my dirty grey tracks a map between black and white. I walk, sleet stinging my face like tears. I wonder if those scientists ever cried, and what happened to those baby monkeys.

Safe Places On Earth

- OSCAR MARTENS -

"No mercy without imagination"
— SOMEBODY

I've been from coast to coast, crossing borders in trucks or rattling motorhomes. I have stolen lunch money, firearms, and clothes from a laundromat dryer. Once I rolled a paperboy. I have been kicked in the head by a hooker I tried to rob in Denver. I lay in the dirt while she squatted over me and washed my cuts with her piss, stuffing a dirty American twenty in my mouth. I am the wrong kind of famous in Montana and Nova Scotia.

My life is rich and meaningless.

Rivers, MB

Combines, seen from the bus window, sweep along the dry prairie stubble, their wide mouths pulling in straight, flat tongues of wheat.

Coming into Rivers in perfect time, the tail end of summer, harvest time, with gears spinning in their hot grease all day, slowing only when the women come in pickups to bring hot meals in tin-foil.

Stepping off the bus into the dusty heat, walking back over the creek, up the hill, down the gravel lane between the windbreak where the dogs begin to bark and run towards me.

Another yard light switches on, another in the kitchen, throwing a square of light onto the yard. Standing on the front steps, hoping the Dycks will remember me from three summers ago.

Mrs. Dyck silent behind the screen door in a shadow while she puts her glasses on. Pushing the door towards me and pulling me into the parallel dimension of the rural Manitoba farmhouse, unchanged from one year to the next, bible verses hanging from small plaques over the kitchen table, butterfly fridge magnets holding up the shopping list, the smells of summer sausage, *zwieback* and *rollkuchen.*

Strangers

There are three types of strangers: the complete stranger, the perfect stranger and the total stranger. I am all of these.

The complete stranger has nothing and that is exactly what he needs. He has appeared and will appear in the future as someone who belongs exactly where he is at any given time.

You don't look twice at his face because he has always been there and when he leaves you will not notice. When he is gone you will not remember.

The perfect stranger is almost always grey and when he is not grey he is beige. These are the primary colours of the man-made world in which he can easily hide.

In order to hide from you, he would sit right next to you while grey thoughts looped in his brain, as he sat with grey posture and matched the grey faces of those around him.

The total stranger is the sum of the parts of his life.

Rivers, MB

The Dycks had enough help for harvest that first summer but they let me do odd jobs like bringing meals to the men or painting fence posts.

I spent time around the house, snooping through their things. In the sewing room, on the top shelf, I found back issues of the *Mennonite Reporter* from '72 on.

There were Mennonites everywhere from Skookumchuck to Madagascar. I had discovered a network of gullible do-gooder pacifists ready to be exploited. The Dycks were delighted with my interest in the Mennonite church.

When I had enough information, I began writing reference letters for myself. I started with names:

Peter Dyck
Irene Friesen
Agnes Paetkau
Bernie Wiens
Henry Loewen
John Rempel
Elmwood Mennonite Church
"Sing to the Lord" Mennonite Choir

Dear Bernie (pastor of target church):

You probably don't remember me but we met at the '82 General Conference in Wichita, Kansas (lie) and participated in a discussion group on "The Healing Power of Christ" (lie). I have fond memories of our fellowship and sharing (big lie).

I am writing this letter to introduce you to John Rempel, a dedicated member of our congregation who has decided to move to Calgary in order to be closer to his sister who is ill (lies, lies, lies).

John has just been through a troubling time (no job, no money, no future) and would appreciate your support (how about a place to stay).

Many Conference members here have spoken of your generosity and unfailing stewardship (meaningless Christian buzzword which will induce guilt if John (me) does not receive assistance).

I'm sure John will benefit greatly from your guidance (implied request and assumption that Bernie will help).

Yours
Sincerely (tee hee),

Henry Loewen
Elmwood Mennonite Church

Language

The alphabet is my best weapon.
It's all there.

↓

abcdefghijklmnopqrstuvwxyz

↑

That's all you need
to slip through bars
or start a holy war.

Mennonite ideology

Mennonites believe in God. I believe in Mennonites, but through my reading I have come to a disturbing revelation. Modern Mennonite faith is based on prudence. The original movement was not. Early converts ran from disgruntled clergy who wanted to stretch them on racks, castrate them with white-hot pincers and scrape out their eyes with wire brushes.

It has become a comfortable religion. Those who met in caves and shared the dangerous new words would be disappointed to find their pale followers clinging to ancient ideals that have become easy to hold, even fashionable.

I doubt that you could sell the religion in its original form.

Believe this, even though they might torture you. Say this, even though you might die. Untested faith leaves them spiritually fat.

Drowning

How could you call it murder? I was holding his head. Underwater. And I kept holding it and I remember it was very hot for early morning and the water was just over my waist in the murky muddy Assiniboine so that I couldn't see him beneath the surface.

How long did I hold him after he had stopped thrashing? Half an hour or an hour? How could it have been anything but peaceful, letting go, letting him drift free of my hands, his hair through my fingers?

Camp

The camp is dark except for one light at the main centre. It's a Mennonite camp, which means that I must stay in the empty counsellors' quarters till midnight, then stumble to her mobile without a flashlight and hiss under her window screen.

In the morning I watch from the arena fence as she drives in horses from pasture, her chin down slightly, warmed by the rough Carhartt, small branches slapping her chinks. She dismounts the horse named 3-10 and begins to cut away horses for the first ride of the day.

An old canner named May, who has become fond of me over the last few days, wanders over to me. Flies eat her eye-sand and I can tell by the lazy way she blinks that she's tired. She moves away when Michelle comes to get her for the ride, but Michelle just keeps walking after her, walking, as I see her patience and love her for it, walking.

Things I miss

1.) My name
2.) The luxury of answering the door
3.) The luxury of answering the phone

4.) The luxury of arousing suspicion

5.) The luxury of telling the truth

6.) The exotic and comforting mediocrity of beef stroganoff, venetian blinds and a full bag of grass clippings by the curb

7.) Credit cards

Fisherman's Wharf

Which one was it? Rows and rows of dumpy plywood shacks that floated. She slowed in the middle of Dock "C" in front of the smallest one, painted like a zebra. It was refreshing or insane, just like the occupant, and as we got on and sent a set of oily ring waves across Fisherman's Wharf I thought of our position on the water, floating on top of something huge, like a water bug must feel on a lake, buoyed by tension only, and that solid land was not real, but rather a large floating raft constantly moving and things were more fragile and temporary than they seemed. I had all those thoughts waiting for Ms. Klassen to unlock the hatch and when she finally did I grabbed her ass with both hands as she bent over to step in and forgot about my lake-bug existence.

Britannia Yacht Club

There's a place where you can go to stand and wait as they pass in their boats. And if you've had a chance to shave and comb your hair and are wearing clothes that aren't obviously dirty, you might be asked to crew. A woman might come over as her boat is being refuelled and invite you onboard.

And moments later you're wrapping rope around a capstan and telling ferocious lies, inventing new extended families and an intricate personal history.

The captain decides to give up the race you have entered. Cutthroat crazy rich people slice past on either side as the helmsman sets a course for the islands where you drop anchor.

Several wine bottles later, you fling the bones of the BBQ chicken overboard and loll about in your fattened state. The anchor is pulled, the sun is setting, a course is set, and the boat is moving slowly, one sail only.

Definitions

Criminal — Not in any way resembling a human. No one you might know or would have raised.

Hardened criminal — Label used to justify any punishment.

Cold-blooded murder — The opposite of hot-blooded murder. Severity of punishment according to temperature of blood. Crime done under influence of childish fit deemed to be less serious regardless of the end result. The incident in Billings was unavoidable. The temperature of my blood was ninety-eight point six degrees.

Correctional institute — The cage, prison, jail, the big-house, the can, the slammer, joint, summer camp, headwaters of Shit Creek, where criminals (see def'n) go to get hardened, fun house, repentance factory, the zoo, hell's waiting room, not a deterrent, not a cure, society's bottom drawer.

Safe places on earth — The only safe place on earth is a coffin.

Regina, SK

I am dining with the parents of the singer I fucked last night. The roast beef is dry, but the meal is saved by a sharp chutney and perfectly roasted carrots. The struggle-with-faith act I used on the girl has similar success with the arrogant ABS, RSP, GIC, PhD father, who assures me that despite his obvious and overwhelming success as a human he too had once doubted the Mennonite faith.

He is preaching about what the scripture clearly tells us while I am thinking about the girl who sits across from me, trying to smell her no-nonsense Christian-white panties, her soap, the excessive baby powder she puffs up into her armpits every morning.

This act is the strongest of my Christian series personas. Being lost invites the target Christian to lead, something which they cannot help themselves from doing. With women it brings out a mothering instinct, especially in those who are in desperate need of mothering themselves.

And so, the concert last night, a Mennonite choir, the scanning of rows of women, their lips making openings of various shapes and sizes, a vulnerable face, a game of eye tag setting us on tracks that will join, compliments after the concert, her suggestion to join the group for coffee, staying at the restaurant until all others had left, my hint about my troubled life, my dilemma, my weakness feeding her strength, my polite and timid manner and the way I stand next to her car in the parking lot, looking like I don't know where I should or could be next, that practised look of no direction, lamb before slaughter, innocent, a look which guarantees access to whatever a victim can offer: a ride, a cup of herbal tea, a comforting hand on the shoulder, pity for my well-timed tears, a comforting hand on the breast, displaced stuffed animals and thick comforters, etc.

I cannot help being impressed by the skills I have developed. My head nods appropriately, my pupils face Our Father, my nose seeks traces of a woman while I appraise the potential post-fence value of the stereo in the living room, Yamaha I think, flirting with me, its decibel band flashing an invitation.

The future

when I reach sixty
I will no longer be able
to deny anything

fingering the holes in my heart
standing with my heart in my hands
fingering the holes and tears

I will be
barefoot on the concrete
standing on every corner at once

The End Of Swinburne

- HARRY TOURNEMILLE -

*"So either the orderliness of nature is where all explanation
stops or we must postulate an agent of great power and knowledge
who brings about, through his continuous actions, that bodies have
the same very general powers and liabilities . . . The simplest such
agent . . . is one of infinite power, knowledge, and freedom, i.e. God."*

— RICHARD SWINBURNE, *The Argument from Design*

That autumn night, everything the moon touched became
bleached bone. The weathered fence-posts, jutting out of
the ground at odd angles, were like the fingers of a dead, buried
giant. Inside the corral, next to a weary barn, where familiar smells
of hay and manure rolled out, I watched Al struggle with an un-
comfortable, pregnant cow. "Necessary unpleasantness," he called
it, but this was nothing new for him. The last cow to give birth had
had the same problem: an anxious calf twisted around, facing the
wrong way. But I watched in relative safety, perched on the fence
with my legs swinging to compensate for jilted nerves. The night
air hurt my lungs whenever I drew a deep breath. Close by, the town
vet — a small, square-headed man with eyes too close together —
leaned up against the barn wall, watching Al's every move. My
father, holding a lit cigarette between burn holes on the index and
third fingers of his black glove, leaned against the fence beside
me. My father always stood close by.

There seemed to be more at stake here than the perils of a breaching calf. Like most ten-year-olds, I learned through experience not to mention the always present adult voices of guidance. Tonight, I was here to witness first-hand God's intimate workings with living beings. Or so my father had told me as we drove up the lazy North Fork road, the headlights of the car casting shadows in the trees.

"The miracle of birth." Dad blew cigarette smoke through the cracked open window. My chest tightened, and my ears burned from the cold. Dad never liked to turn the heat on.

"How's it a miracle if it happens all the time?" I exhaled, trying to make my own smoke, and had to make do with writing my initials on the fogged passenger window.

"Because God doesn't allow for accidents."

My throat ached with frustration.

—

Farming flowed through Al's veins. It was in his blood from birth, fed through his umbilical cord from work boots, flannel shirts, Larry Norman record albums, and his Bible. This is how he understood the world: he filtered ideas through his fingers, scratched the surface of the ground with his clipped and filed nails, looking for evidence, ideas. He would plunge his hands deep into the garden just to feel the pulse of the earth. They were complex hands, capable of pounding fence posts into the ground all afternoon, or cleaning out the carburetor on one of the work trucks. But they were also gentle hands, hands that found the small of his wife's back or picked up his three-year-old, tottering daughter.

My father had similar hands: bony, powerful, familiar with knowledge of soil. But his complexities were different. Forged of discipline and a childhood at the receiving end of anger, his hands were quick to strike in spite of all the good in his heart. But these same hands also held me on his lap in the bathroom one night when I was shaking with fever, cradled me while steam rolled over the top of the shower curtain, into my lungs, loosening up the phlegm so I could breathe again.

My father's hands were burdened by having to do so much to please God: giving marrow and knuckle for an ethereal embrace. I could tell it wore him out, the sadness around his eyes always masked by a need to please. He wanted to be a vessel, wanted God to work through his human hands. Wanted it because he thought it would bring comfort, the promise of future glory for all his damned misery. On Sunday mornings, my father would thrust his hands high into the air just to see if God was there. I would glower and sink down into the musty church pew, curling my hands into fists, thrusting them deep into my pockets.

—

I leaned forward, trying to hear the vet's low voice as he spoke to Al, his thick fingers pushing thin, wire glasses onto the bridge of his nose. Al nodded at what he heard and rolled the sleeve on his right arm up to the shoulder. He grabbed a length of stainless steel chain from a bucket of hot, soapy water and held it up for inspection. Fingers of steam crept up the links. Dad placed a hand on the back of my head. I could hear his raspy breathing, could smell the tension seeping from his pores. His nervousness was spreading to me, and I drummed the fence with my heels. With his arm soaped up, Al looked at me and winked. I smiled back — until he began easing first his hand, then his entire arm, into the cow's birth canal. The response was immediate: a strained bellow from the tethered cow, and then a shower of feces, urine and blood soaked Al from head to foot.

"Shit!" Al shot a fine spray from his lips.

The stench reminded me of when I used to ride my bicycle past the town sewage plant during summer. The air was so heavy and thick with smell I thought I could taste it. I giggled through my hands and felt the one on my neck tighten. I knew my father was frowning.

"You just never mind that," he said.

—

Dad was always trying to enlighten me about God, as if it were his duty to give proof of every detail. A school teacher, he thought he had to teach me — even on weekends, but perhaps he needed to convince himself more than anything else. I was young, easily seduced by stories of power and wrath and mercy, easily convinced that the unseen moved over the surface of the earth. But for Dad, it was different. He had to repeat things over and over and over, until he believed them, or until they at least became habit. Sometimes, he just plain gave up for awhile, only to come back later to try again.

Years earlier, allegations came out that a teacher in my elementary school had molested many of the young girls in his class over a span of ten years. My father testified and after the trial was over, he sagged with weariness. For weeks he said little, never lifted his eyes to heaven once. He was healing himself, I suspect, resigned to the fact that he was on his own this time. I would watch him in his recliner, those active hands folded across his stomach, too tired now to do anything but interlace and support one another. He'd sit with his eyes closed, or look out the living room window, and sigh from time to time. It was the same sigh I heard so many times when I'd done something to disappoint him, an exhale escaping through the cracks of a fragmented, hurting soul. The sound of failure.

—

Al had called us out for this visit because the pregnant cow had finally found her way close enough to the farm house to be corralled. Usually Al had to hop on a quad or his tractor and roam the woods to find the mother. Once they started giving birth, they would just stay put no matter where they were. A few years back, he couldn't get to one of the cows in time and the calf asphyxiated, breaching half way out. The cow spooked when the calf stopped moving, and ran to the farthest corners of the eighteen-hundred-acre ranch. Al didn't find her until it was too late. The dangling calf started to decompose and the mother went into toxic shock, leaving Al with no choice but to go back to the quad, get out his rifle, and put the suffering mother down. His voice sounded heavy whenever he told that story; some things evaded God, some things were just brute facts.

Tonight was different though. Aside from doing cartwheels that ended feet down, this calf seemed to be in fine shape. Dad explained to me that Al was trying to loop one end of the chain around the calf's hooves so he could turn it around, bring the front legs out first. *A part of God's perfect plan,* he said to comfort me. I thought Al was groping around blind, with an outstretched arm, looking for something, anything.

"Boy, come down here and take a look, quick though," Al called.

Dad released his hold on my neck, and I slid down the fence, reaching with my feet until my shoes found hay and earth. I walked up to where Al squatted beside the soap bucket.

"You're brave, aren't you?"

"Yes." A white lie, a little sin.

"Some strange things goin' on, huh?"

I nodded, feeling little tremors in my legs and abdomen.

"Well, if you want to learn about something, you gotta use your hands. So, come over here and grab onto this chain."

I didn't move. The cow was fidgeting.

"Hey." Al looked up at me this time, serious, but not angry. "I'm not going to force you to do it. You take stock and then decide." He wiped his forehead with his forearm. "What'll it be?"

I took the chain into my nervous fingers. The steel, slick with fluids and smells, writhed in my hands, but I gripped it tight, wrestling it for a grip. Al joined the vet back at the cow and called over his shoulder.

"Okay, now I want you to pull strong and steady. No jerking, 'cause we don't want to freak the ol' girl out here; real smooth, okay?"

I did as he asked and as Al and my father shouted their praises, I wondered what Christ Almighty was doing in a cow's dark and ominous regions. Another one of those things I couldn't keep track of: the elusive wanderings of the Holy Ghost. The mother cow had gone all quiet, like she realized that Al was inside her for the right reasons. Then, a squelching sound — what you hear in your head when you squeeze Jell-o through your teeth with your mouth closed — and neat as can be, a slithery lump of life plopped onto the hay. The mother sank to the ground exhausted. I gagged out loud.

The vet rushed over to inspect the calf, his gloved hands probing and lifting, clearing the airway with a turkey baster. He nodded and then went back to the mother who had been allowed to rest on her side until now. It would be real tough on her heart if she lay down for too long, so he had to drive his knees into her ribs three or four times until she finally struggled upright. The calf was busy as well, trying to get up on its own rickety, folding-chair legs. After three or four tries, and a few nudges from Al's boot, the little suckler wobbled over to its trembling mother, went straight to the teats and starting guzzling. Al said that happened most of the time, *instinct* he called it. The mother was responding according to her instincts as well, craning her neck and trying to nuzzle the newborn to keep it warm in the piercing night air.

The moon was bright enough to illuminate everything. The worklight Al had suspended from the rafters had little effect. He ducked around the side of the barn to hose off as best he could. I watched the moon, thinking of when Dad took me to the night baseball games at the park. Those huge lamps that lit the field were brighter than sunlight, leaving everything exposed. The moon seemed the same way, sharp and invasive. I looked at my father, who was a few metres out into the pasture. He was watching the moon as well, feeble wraiths of smoke playing around his head. Some of the people in the church had mentioned my father's smoking at one of their meetings, meetings where they got together to spit and hiss at the world. *Desecration of one's temple,* they called it. But for now, everything was silent, covered in frosted glass under a bitter light.

Al came around from the side of the barn, his crusty shirt now replaced with a grey work coat that he kept on a hook in one of the stalls. He moved beside me and leaned over the fence, resting his chin on his forearms. Areas behind his ears and on the back of his neck were still flecked with cow shit. Steam rose from the pen as we listened to the frantic suckling of the calf. I studied my dry, tacky hands. I could feel the visceral connection between life and my sense of touch, but I couldn't piece it together, couldn't artic- ulate it, not yet. I felt like I was a part of something then, something unidentifiable.

The vet had packed up his bag by this time and climbed out of the corral. He shook Al's hand, smiled at me, and headed back to his truck to make the long trek back into town. Al looked ex- hausted, but there were little crinkles of satisfaction around his eyes and mouth.

"That was a little bit of rock and roll, now wasn't it?"

I shrugged and picked at a knot-hole in one of the logs.

"This," he said, "is real life." He scratched behind one of his ears, noticed the mess still there, and wiped it on his pant leg. "This is how everything works, all part of nature, yet part of something more."

"More what?" I turned to look at him.

"Nature and the divine, man, nature and the divine." He tugged my left ear. "You done real good tonight."

I concentrated on the toes of my boots.

"Why did we have to use the chain, though?"

My father, amidst several deep, chest-wracking coughs, came back to join us. His eyes squinted a little, but he smiled at Al.

"Isn't it amazing what happens in the hand of God?" he said. "There is so much . . ."

We all stood still, Dad and Al feeling affirmed by what had hap- pened. I looked down at my hands again, studied the creases, the lifelines, and tried to massage some warmth into my cold fingers. Above me nothing moved.

Counting Chickens

- RON J. WIEBE -

"The Andreeson quarter got a whole foot." Al Bedard's hands suck heat from his coffee cup. Across the table, his father Wilbur exhales and squints into the smoke curling under the greasy brim of his Cockshutt hat. They watch Mrs. Chu's headscarf bob above the frost wave on the window as she shovels the snow in front of Chu's E-lite Café.

"The Andreeson quarter — reminds me of harvest, year before you'se born," says Wilbur.

"Mmm." Al has heard the story dozens of times in his twenty-three years. He regrets mentioning the Andreeson land, named for its homesteaders, that he and his father farm.

Slippers clap to their table. Wing Chu tops up their mugs, thick and chipped, with scalded coffee, best in town. "Hot Saskatoon pie frozen-fresh?" They nod and he slap-slaps away.

Al redirects the conversation. "Snow'll hold up seeding."

Wilbur spins the Carnation Milk can between the thumb and remaining three fingers of his right hand. "Work a the Almighty, that's what your mother says we seen that day." He grins at Al. "Or maybe Beelzebub."

"Yup, we'll be considerable late on the land this spring."

"Prob'ly put us into frost at harvest," Wilbur concedes and they invoke the farmer's rite of acknowledging the dangerous blessing of moisture on the land.

"And into the Co-op for more money. They already own most of us."

"'Cept for Hulda and Adolph. They've been free and clear for years." Wilbur bites off the words, as he always does when he talks about Hulda and Adolph Hiebert.

—

Adolf Hiebert came from late-immigration Russian Mennonite stock. His parents had spent the Canadian portion of their lives squeezing a few bushels of wheat from the stony ground of a left-over Saskatchewan homestead. Daily, the elder Hieberts had read the scriptures. Regularly, they had dourly cleaved unto each other and in due course they had raised up a bountiful crop of barefoot children whom they firmly encouraged to rid the land of rocks. Within a generation, the land was picked almost clean of these offspring who had escaped to higher education or life insurance sales.

But Adolph stuck to farming. Twenty-three years ago he had abandoned his parents' hopeless homestead and married money in the generously proportioned form of Hulda Hayes of the wealthy Feedlot Hayes. The newlyweds purchased good land by the South Saskatchewan River and joined the optimistic Praise-the-Lord Gospel Church of Truth and Light.

Seven months after the wedding, Hulda was exactly seven months pregnant, give or take a week. And lo, she received a sign from the Lord. Anxiously, she waited for Sunday so she could share it.

That Sunday happened to be Amplify-Your-Faith Sunday — the unveiling of the church's new sound system. The sound technology idea had come to Preacher Ulrich direct from the Lord; the flash had struck twice just a few blocks apart. Three weeks earlier, the New Modern Bible Church, meeting in the flat-roofed Odd Fellows Hall, had also become amplified.

Between these two churches rose the spire of St. Mary's where Wilbur Bedard and his pregnant wife Viola worshipped. St. Mary's, it seemed, was grounded against heavenly arcing. Its Mass continued unamplified and unremarkable between the competing pillars of praise rising from the New Moderns and the Truth-and-Lighters.

Pastor Ulrich, on that first amplified Sunday, symbolically sprinkled baptismal water on the microphone — things electrical being exempt from full immersion. The speakers squawked out sanctified feedback when he announced, "The Co-op Credit Union is giving the Lord prime plus two and a year to pay the sound system loan which the Board of Elders guaranteed personal. We're counting on the Lord to bring in the harvest. I just feel the Spirit leading someone to prophesy and pledge the first hundred dollars to the Amplify-Your-Faith Fund, so you'd best say it now lest the blessing be withheld from thee." Hulda's hand shot up.

Elder Martin snaked the cord through the faithful to bring Hulda the mortgaged microphone. "Well it's me and Adolph making that first pledge," she said, "because just Thursday I was about to cook up Adolph's favourite, those Captain Highliner fish sticks, praise the Lord, and the Bible's on top of the fridge, right? And we've been naming and claiming the promise of God, 'And whatsoever we ask, we shall receive . . .' Amen? So we're counting on the Lord for the first of four Christian sons to help farm and all.

"Well, my back's shot, being in the family way, and I must not a put that Bible back there far enough, because when I open the freezer and reach for Captain Highliner, the Bible she falls open on the floor, but I don't think nothing except pick it up quick because floor dirt and God's Holy Word don't mix, and the floor's dirty, right, since floor-washing buggers my back. So I bend down quick, one hand still ahold of the fish sticks cause everything in the freezer is depending on them to stay put and sure enough my back locks up tighter than an old maid's — excuse me Mabel — and I'm bent over with my head on the fridge door, one hand down on God's Word and one trying to hold things together up above, cause if one thing goes she all goes — right? Finally I remember Christ's words — let go and let God — so I do. And the frozen pot roast clips me a good one on the back a the head. Ice cubes and everything is falling like hail and I can't hold my bearings. I tip backwards hard, back still locked-up, sit down smack solid and my down below area goes whoosh! 'Well, that's what it's like when your waters break,' I think. 'It sure is cold.' But then I find it's just the ice cream tub I sat on — Co-op Chocolate Ripple."

If there was one thing Elder Martin knew for sure, it was that he and God did not approve the mention of down-below-areas or breaking-waters, especially in The House of the Lord. So he jigged the cord to signal Hulda to shut it down. But Hulda held fast. Elder Martin, new to the art of microphone retrieval, turned his attention to the other end of things, hoping for one goodly yank to unplug the cord. The cord had run up between the bony knees and over the shoulder of senile Mrs. Spenst, who slept at the front in her wheel chair. Feeling the cord tighten, she awoke and held on for dear life, thinking it was the Cord of the Lord come to tow her Home. The Elder, unaware of what he had snagged, heaved hard into the cord, so that Mrs. Spenst, whose rear brakes were on, did a holy wheely right there at the altar, and when her front wheels left the ground she knew for sure it was the Second Coming of Christ, which she'd been counting on for years. She cackled and whooped and released herself because she was ready to go.

Hulda remained behind. "Well, I'm bent over the Bible that's laying open between my knees, mostly covered in Chocolate Ripple but words just sort of jump out: 'For I have borne him a son . . .' and then I knew for sure I could claim that promise for a son. Sometimes it sure takes a lot of commotion for the Lord to get our attention. We're having the pot roast today."

Six weeks later, the baby was born.

—

Outside Wing Chu's Café, it is snowing again. Wilbur Bedard and his son Al smoke and watch Mrs. Chu's metronoming broom.

"Remember what's-her-name, that kid of Hulda and Adolph's?" asks Wilbur.

"Sarah. She was some wild." Al twists the ends of another roll-your-own.

"Yeah, she was your age. Started hitching when she was eleven. RCMP brung her back. Off she'd go again. Finally, when she's fourteen Hulda says, 'Don't be bringing her back here.'"

"We kids figured Hulda knew Sarah was knocked up," says Al.

After Sarah had ripped herself from Hulda's womb, Hulda aimed her wind-chilled wrath at God and Adolph for this trick. She flung the Bible into an unused barn stall. She presented Adolph with charred fish sticks and crossed thighs. This disappointed Adolph. He punished God by farming Sundays.

They quit church. When the Elders visited to remind them of their Amplify-Your-Faith pledge "because the New Moderns got their system paid and upgraded even but the Lord got left holding our bag and what does that look like?" Hulda held up screaming Sarah and said, "Amplify this, goddammit." Silently, the Elders left.

The Hieberts farmed bitterly, beating the land into wheat production. Occasionally Adolph used the unused barn stall to spill his seed, until six-year-old Sarah spied him through a knothole and screamed more loudly than usual. Hulda whipped Sarah for what she had seen and told Adolph she was taking over running things since he couldn't keep both hands to the plough.

Hulda Hiebert was a business natural. When neighbours struggled financially, Hulda found the means to buy their land. Invariably, under Hulda's ownership, the fickle land would burst forth into bumper crops. No one knew why. In twenty or so years, the

Hieberts had accumulated three-and-a-half sections of mortgage-free land.

"Yeah, now they're sitting pretty every winter in Arizona." Wilbur takes off his hat and pokes at his bald head, which is starkly white compared to his rawhide face. "And them twenty years junior to me 'n Viola." The orange neon sign above them flashes "Cheap Eats."

"Hiebert's been pouring on the chemicals, last three years. Got nothing in summer-fallow. They'll milk it for everything, then start to fallow as if nothing was wrong and sell off to InterGrain Inc. for a million or so." Al holds up two fingers for pie.

—

The Hieberts' Arizona trailer park mornings are spent arguing over The Price is Right. Hulda has learned the cost of everything. This morning, Adolph, a buck seventy-five over on a box of Tide, gets up and goddamns his way outside. Hulda knits and talks to the TV. "Seven ninety-nine, you stupid bugger!" — clickity-click — "Jeez-Louise, you're way over." Clickity-click, click.

Adolph hates the sound of Hulda's knitting. He despises the useless rippled pelts with malformed appendages that crawl from the needles and hibernate in piles all over the motor home. When the TV is off, Hulda knits and cries.

On the shady side of the neighbouring motor home, Adolph drinks beer and talks gas mileage and next year's crop failure with Ben Oglarski, the Old Fart — that's what it says on his hat. Ben is a retired Ukrainian farmer, a widower, who collects Hunky jokes and grandchildren. He pulls out a walletful of grandkids' pictures and proudly tells Adolph how useless they all are. "Especially this one, she's going in for doctoring — not your normal sick kind, so what good is that? And then there's this little bugger here, plays rep hockey, no-good-for-nuthin' little pain-in-the-ass, don't he look like me?" Then he says to Adolph, "Hey, you heard the one about the Hunky that showed everyone the picture of the kid that come with his wallet, eh?"

Adolph always leaves his wallet inside.

From next door they hear Bob Barker say, "Come on down!"

—

Wing Chu brings pie for Wilbur and Al. He taps on the window, and chatters at his wife. She ignores him.

Wilbur says, "Yup, lost the whole crop, best I ever seen . . ."

"Over on the Andreeson land." Al surrenders to the story. "Year before I was born. And you never sold it off. Could of . . ." Al is puzzled by his parents' obsession with this one story. They had lost other crops.

His father takes over. "Could a though. Hulda made me some good offers." He talks at the window. "Course, for your mother it might as well be holy ground, so we just kept paying the mortgage all these years. Hook or by crook. At least that quarter's finally paid off."

Unaware of this, Al looks up at his father.

"Time you heard the whole thing," says Wilbur. He smiles at his reflection, remembering.

—

Harvest, twenty-four years ago. The rusted Massey combine floats wheel-deep in a high-tide wash of number one hard red wheat. Wilbur Bedard walks toward the larboard-listing old half-ton at the edge of the field, figuring on supper before starting in on this Andreeson quarter. He snaps off a flaxen head, counts the rows of kernels. He mills its crispness into his callused palm, reckoning thirty/thirty-five bushels to the acre, which he's never seen ever in his forty-four years. He offers the chaff to the wind and tosses the wheat into his mouth, milling it with farmer's teeth ground half to the gum.

Wilbur feels so blessed that he guns the pickup the half-mile home, the loose fender bounding off the tire. He brakes by the chicken coop in a dusty cloud of clucks and barks, coming up behind Viola, his wife, bent over gathering fine brown eggs from Hector their best layer. He slides his rough three-fingered hand between Viola's plump thighs so that the startled eggs leap from her apron and tomorrow's breakfast is pecked up by a dozen fat hens. But Wilbur doesn't notice or care because of where his hand is and the news he has: "We're going to Hawaii!! Just like I promised!" He had promised every year since they were married, to make up for no children. But it had never worked out. They giggle and tickle to the house, barely making it to the upstairs bedroom, where they make love like honeymooners — except they know their way around — and great slappings of air gasp out from between them, raising up puffs of chicken down and grain dust shot through with the sun stream from the west window, so that there is a golden-feathered cloud surrounding them — as if they are in heaven.

Afterwards, Wilbur, naked and smelling of sex, rushes downstairs. He phones Co-op Travel over in Saskatoon before they close. He books the last two discount seats. Nonrefundable.

Viola calls. He grins, counting on seconds. When he enters the bedroom, she is standing naked, looking out the west window. She is fingering the cross between her breasts. And he knows. He holds her and they watch the cloud that has come, etched in white heat, roiling the smoke of its mile-high head. They watch the shear edge of the white bullet sheet approach. The hail consumes the garden one row at a time, neat as a mower. It pauses. Ten feet from the window it pauses. It can stop if it wishes. The power examines their nakedness. Viola crosses herself. Then hammers anneal their roof, driving the lovers with awful fascination to the other window. In fifteen minutes the hail harvest of the Andreeson land is over. The combine stands unskirted. Wilbur's half-tanned arms slip from Viola's slumped shoulders. He brings her robe.

That night, holding each other brings a sad lovemaking. As he does every night, Wilbur falls asleep to Viola's clicking rosary. She murmurs, "Glory be to the Father, and to the Son, and to the Holy Spirit, as it was in the beginning, is now, and ever shall be, world without end. Amen."

Wilbur looks from his reflection to his only child. "Nine months later, you show up. Your mother says, 'You can't never tell reaping from sowing. It's a puzzlement.' Anyhow, that Andreeson quarter, it's yours, if you should want. Me and your mother sort a been counting on you taking over."

Al watches Mrs. Chu. Eddies of new snow have rounded the corners of her squared-off patch. She leans on her shovel, considering the sky. A sighed-out breath cloud momentarily hides her face. Al scrapes at the last of his pie filling, leaving a purple tongue of crust. "This kind of snow, we'll be two weeks late to seeding for sure. Maybe three."

"If she don't flood," says his father.

Poetry

Faspa

- CARLA FUNK -

My dad arrives home Sunday after a weekend
hunting trip, bull moose with ten-point antlers

strapped to the back of his pickup,
Jack pine and oil scent in his clothes.

In the driveway, I hold the animal's mouth open
for him to cut out its tongue, knife-blade

at the back of the throat, his hands slow and gentle.
We carry it in a clean towel to the house,

wash it in the kitchen sink. He shows me how
to peel out the roots and leave the meat,

drain the blood without taking away the taste.
He boils it in saltwater, steam clouding the stove,

and I set two places at the table, forks, knives, plates.
Two small bowls of vinegar and sugar.

He divides it between us, three slices each,
and we take turns dipping each mouthful,

first vinegar, then sugar, sting and sweet.
I try to eat slowly enough to make it last.

Faspa: A traditional late-afternoon Sunday lunch

Bums

- CARLA FUNK -

Big bums are hereditary
in my family, passed down
from mother to daughter
like the knack to bake
a perfect apple pie.

Not just wide bums, but
fleshy, plump, pillowy bums. Bums
white as cumulous clouds, white as
two polar bears hugging. Bums
dimpled and powdery as snowfall,
smooth and supple as bread dough
rising in loaves on warm kitchen counters.

My mother says our bums go as far back
as my great-great-grandmother Fanny,
(yes, that really was her name)
who passed down the recipe
for her famous maple cookies,
and the largesse of her bottom. The size,
I'm told, of a prize-winning pumpkin, half-
hidden under layers of petticoat.

From Fanny to her daughter Lily
to my grandmother Barbara
to my mother to me. We complain
about its size, how everything we eat

goes right to our bottoms, how the seams
in our skirts always need letting out but —
there are no bums like ours
for sitting. They give way
for the rest of our weight
like feather-filled cushions, shape
us like pears on the family tree.

Angel of Stupidity

- CARLA FUNK -

For the kid who licks the frozen tetherball post in February.

For the boy who stares into the barrel of his gun
to see how far down the pellet rests.

For the girl who practises her pogo-stick
on the high and rail-less deck, there is this angel —

bold-winged, brazen and dependable,
part lifeguard, part paramedic,
part SWAT team dispatcher.

For the bored youth who lines
the railroad tracks with dimes, just to see
whether the stories of tragic train wrecks
come true, this angel bends down,
with its wing-tip flips the coin off.

For the girl who accepts a ride home from the gravel pit party
with a guy whose pickup spins eternal gravel, whose fingernails
creased with grease tap the dash in time to Megadeath,
whose best joke involves her the morning after,
this angel pulls the spark plug, punctures
the tire with a sharp quill.

For the man who takes a run from the top of the cliff
in a homemade hang-glider, having skimmed
the instructions in a language he does not speak,
this angel tangles a length of rope around the foolish ankle.

For the woman who climbs the highest branch
of her orchard's apple tree, pruning
shears aimed against the target of her heart,
this angel waits at the bottom, wings hovering
like a safety net, ready to ease
the timeless, predictable fall.

On the Banning of Beauty

- CARLA FUNK -

"During the days of the Great Proletarian Cultural Revolution
in China in the 1960s, Chairman Mao dismissed
beauty as a bourgeois concept. Red Guards closed flower
shops and ordered people to destroy their goldfish . . ."

— PHILLIP YANCEY, *Rumours of Another World*

Lock the gates against splendour,
black out every luxury and pleasure —
tear from the country's lexicon the word *lovely*.

Call beauty an infection,
and it only spreads,
roots deeper in the earth.

In the uniform streets, people on bicycles
pedal out whole dynasties of verse,
each downward foot a poem's stressed syllable
pumping forward through silence.

In the oil and steam of the factories,
workers compose love songs for bells and drums,
make of the mind a rebel orchestra pit.

No silk threads embroidering their slippers
with phoenix, lotus, a dragon's fire, the women
find other ways to burn. Behind the drawn curtains
of their shadowed houses, they hang
polished teaspoons from the ceiling,
catch what light they can
from the candles' glow.

Children, knowing the laws by which they are governed,
hide marbles under loose floorboards,
cover the glass bowls of goldfish with dark cloth
and slide them under the beds.
While they sleep, scales flicker beneath,
stowaway cells of a dreamworld waiting
to be woken and entered.

Under the muted palette of night,
across the city and in another room,
a man's hand traces the body of his beloved,
his finger a brush that paints her skin
with the calligraphy of bamboo and plum,
all the flesh alive, a hundred flowers blooming.

Nightwalk

- CARLA FUNK -

Sky's black gloss and the street
a long mirror of sidewalk lights.

The wind pushes wet leaves and an empty
garbage bag slick with rain behind you

and your dark neighbourhood shakes
the folded map inside.

What makes the body pace
the night to sudden nowhere,

the feet wear down the earth's hard edges.
So the idea begins its slow erosion from stone.

Like the artist with his prophet hands
sculpting slabs of marble sliver-thin,

a father's hand on his small girl's forehead
the wound soothed down to sleep

or Jesus' naked back sanding down
the wood's rough cut smooth as bone.

The blood with its desert silt pours on
in the anxious cities,

in you who walks the darkness
with that hand upon your shoulder

to wear away the heaviness
to usher down the flesh.

Revelations, Age Eight

- CARLA FUNK -

The number of the beast was enough
to scare anyone especially when Uncle Wayne preached
of European plans to tattoo the digit
666 on the forehead of every consumer

take the number and go to hell
or brave the tribulation as a true follower
starving in the end times wasteland

I pictured me   my brother and mom
with bloated bellies   stick arms and legs
drinking mouthfuls of snow
foraging for rosehips and tree bark
desperate for the rapture
with my equally devout relatives
hollow-eyed cousins   gaunt aunts and uncles

and what would become of my father
who hadn't been to church in years
though he choked up Sundays at 4 p.m.
whenever Tommy Hunter sang the old hymns

those evenings he'd pull his harmonica
from the junk drawer
run his mouth over the hollow teeth
in a rusty version of *Jesus Loves Me*

his eternity my dilemma
knowing he couldn't go a day without his Export A's
knowing he'd believe the apocalypse a sham
would march on down to the bank or Co-op or village office
wherever a guy had to go to get that beastly mark
and me quietly grateful for his lack of faith
selling him out for a can of mushroom soup
a box of crackers

together our family at the kitchen table
straddling the fault line
between paradise and damnation
my father's feet in the fire
the rest of us already eating the banquet

Doxology

- CARLA FUNK -

To him who is able to keep me from falling
the way I fell at age five down the chimney
of our half-built house   came to stumbling
in the skeleton outlines of basement walls
until the carpenter scooped me up
and carried me to my mother who stood
paralyzed in the strawberry patch

To him who is able to mend the broken places
like my collarbone floating loose
under the doctor's cold hands   my split forehead
draped with black cloth and sewn closed
by the careful nurse's stinging stitch

To him who is able to cover all shame
and naked embarrassment when on the way
home from the hospital my father insisted
on stopping at the neighbour's house
to show them this accident and me
wearing nothing but underwear
shivering in the front seat of the pickup
while George Jones and Tammy Wynette
crooned their duet love on the radio
and the neighbours clucked their tongues
through the driver's side window

To him who is able to present me faultless before the throne
and before the mirror where I stood daily
watching my two black eyes change
purple to green to jaundiced yellow
and fingering the notch in my crooked shoulder
the black thread in my swollen brow

To him who is able to trade ashes for beauty
carve from the cracked bone unearthly scrimshaw
lace light through the skin of the uneven scar

Midnight in the Bedroom

- CARLA FUNK -

Window cracked open to the sound of late summer
crickets, it begins with the hunchback and the
cantaloupe-sized goitre — which would you rather have? —
a question sprung on the verge of sleep, that space
where the brain gallops off across the black wilderness
in search of adventure, a stampede of wild mustangs, fire.

And you, turning over in bed, choose the goitre,
say at least you could paint it up like a second head,
wrap a scarf around it, name it, stroke it publicly
in supermarket line-ups, give the bored cashiers
something to talk about after a long shift.
Goitres, you say, hold mystery,
have cachet in an iodine-rich society.

Like the man in my childhood hometown
standing across from me in the local Co-op produce aisle,
his hand gripping a honeydew or a head of cabbage,
that dark red bulge on the back of his neck.
"The guy with the goitre," our family called him,
beige corduroy blazer, thin wisps combed over
to cover his baldness, though who would ever notice
his thinning hair in light of that goitre.

I never learned his name, but he looked like
a Stanley or a Harold, the kind of man who might
spend evenings bent over his stamp collection,
a quiet philatelist listening to Bert Kaempfert
and his orchestra play *Cha Cha Brasilia* or
Red Roses for a Blue Lady. The music
a Stanley or Harold would love.

Not the music of a Ron or a Ted, which would be
altogether different, Bob Seger and the Silver Bullet
Band, Boston and Steely Dan cranked up on a back deck
party night with Labatt Blue from the bottle and not the can,
hot tub foaming middle-aged women in two-piece swimsuits
though their bodies have sagged far past that idea, but
Ron or Ted and their yard full of friends don't mind,
still hoot smoky laughter at the moon and hold
cigarette lighters to the suburban sky.

But you are not a Stanley or a Harold, not a Ron or a Ted,
you are a Lance who does not collect stamps or drink beer —
still, if you had to slap your money down in a pub,
what would a Lance ask for — Blue Velvet Martini,
Desert Sunrise, Vermouth Cocktail?

Though you've pulled your pillow over your head,
I can tell you're thinking about how a name determines
one's place in the world, tattoos the soul's signature
onto every first impression one gives.

And if you had to change your name, for example, to Gene
or Merle or Hank, would you wear a cowboy hat, dusty
boots and a twelve-string guitar slung over your shoulder,
would you carry in your heart a soundtrack of wild
hoof beats and lonesome harmonica, sing
sad goodbyes in the campfire's light.

Would you lie beside me on your midnight bedroll,
one slow hand holding onto my hip, the sound of crickets
stitching the moon to the dark, would you listen to
these questions that spark and flicker, would you
stay awake long enough to answer.

Epiphany

- CARLA FUNK -

For some it comes like cresting
a hilltop on bicycle to find
the slow purple horizon,
a pleasant coast into consciousness.

For some it's a telegram that drops to the table
from the messenger's shaking hand.

Or it's the smoke alarm shrieking burnt toast
over the heart's morning colic.

For others it's a butcher chucking
a ham hock down onto brown paper
sudden and brutish as the stained apron
upon which he smears his hands.

And for the newlywed young woman
who steps into this butcher's shop
to purchase a tender cut for her man,
it grips the heart's most vital valve,
all those brilliant slabs of flesh
hung like lanterns above her head,
her wedding night a flash of heat
in the body's most delicate mechanism.

In cartoons it's a light bulb burst above
the brain, the idea causing the fingers to snap
then a blur of rush lines as the character zooms
off screen while our cartoonist holds a dull pencil
above the blank page, waits for his own illumination.

A revelatory manifestation of a divine being
says the dictionary, thinking back to the camels
sulking over months' worth of desert, the wise men
who knelt at the foot of the boy Jesus,
their hands lifting to stroke the dark
head of God, a wound that infects
every gesture after.

I'll take mine any way I can get it,
anything for a flame in night's black tunnel,
anything for a feast in the winter's bleak light.

Borscht

- BARBARA NICKEL -

This is what Oma learned in Russia, 1918:

Boil beef or mutton bones with water, vinegar, salt.

If Nestor Mahkno and his bandits steal 6,000 rubles, offer borscht.

Late tomatoes, sprigs of dill . . .

Liebet eure Feinde, tut Gutes denen, die euch hassen,
und betet für sie, die euch verfolgen.

If they rape your daughters, burn your estate . . .

(Broth becomes richer with each reheating.)

Liebet eure Feinde . . . : "Love your enemies, pray for those who persecute
you" (Matthew 5:44).

Manifesto

- BARBARA NICKEL -

*"We allow and give Leave for all Foreigners to come into Our Empire,
the vast Lands, unexhaustable Treasures hidden in the Bosom of the Earth —
to settle in the open Fields, in Colonys or by Places,
to build themselves up Churches with steeples for Bells."*
— CATHERINE II, Manifesto of 1763

You made me when you stepped from the sleigh into the snow.
Moscow unknown to you, fourteen, foreigner about to meet
the Empress. Your mother and you, *six weeks on the way . . .*
the journey . . . long, very tiresome, and harrowing. With swollen feet,
about to meet a husband who turned gargoyle
and strange. The palaces prison. Nights, the fire
spit German syllables — *Liebchen,* your father's goodbye, those
    falling
stars as your coach moved away. Homeless, you built
houses of words. Empress, you opened this door:
We allow and give Leave for all Foreigners to come into Our Empire.

On your steppe my people unloaded doctrines, deacons,
history of persecutions. Industrious. Neat. You prized
them like colonies of pearls. Safe in the orchard, hymn, home,
tight little village turned in on itself,
a man sitting by the fire might hear it rupture —
just wood caving in — but in that, the future: births
and births forward, Aunt Mary's voice on the tape, telling
about the revolution, mid-story, falters. I pressed pause.
She couldn't go on. Her table laid for *faspa* set forth
the vast lands, inexhaustible treasures hidden in the bosom of the earth —

madrigal of aspen and grasses by the river, a whole ravine
in a spoon of Saskatoon jam. Beet pickles, *ikra,* platters

of sausage and ham. What settled among us, then, sifted past
the clatter of dishes and chatter? Dusk, summer,
frog chorus through the open window as we sang
grace — she ladled, poured, replenished, her face
suffused with suffering and love. Family around
a table. I wanted more. You made me when you stepped
from the sleigh into the snow, not by letting us
settle in the open fields, in colonies or by places

I've never seen. Wrote Voltaire, *You are . . . the brightest*
star . . . Not fixed for my gazing on your heroic
furthering of my people but swirling —
gaseous, dense and deep — igniting motion: a step,
a coup, coronation, a strangling, building, razing,
burning, journeying on, over the Dnieper's rills
to Moscow, or by car to Great Deer over the old Borden bridge
(collapsed now) to stand by Aunt Mary's grave.
Even here presses the stellar wind,
building up churches with steeples for bells.

"Manifesto" is excerpted from "Empress," a longer series of glosas about
Catherine II. Known as Catherine the Great (1729–1796), she ruled from
1762–1796, one of the longest reigns in Russian history. With no legal
claim to the Russian crown, she overthrew her husband in a coup six
months after he became tsar. Her guards murdered him a week later.

The borrowed quatrains for the glosas are adapted from prose material
about Catherine.

The quote for "Manifesto" is adapted from the official English-language
version of Catherine's Manifesto of 1763, found in Roger Bartlett's *Human*
Capital: The settlement of foreigners in Russia 1762–1804. The italicized phrases
"six weeks on the way. . ." etc. in the first stanza are Catherine's, from her
memoirs.

My Brother's Wedding Ring

- BARBARA NICKEL -

clinked on the steering wheel of the old station wagon as he
    drove north
to our cabin for his honeymoon. He told me he noticed this
    because as a kid, sitting
in the back seat of the same car, viewing out the window the
    same but younger
blur of pine, he'd heard Dad's ring clink like that. I can imagine
my brother

amidst sandwich-making, arm-twisting, the eight-track playing
    Dr. Seuss and
the Beach Boys, amidst howls, farts, giggles, threats (*you keep that
    up and I'll make you*
run behind awhile) and that gas-plastic-mustard smell heating up
    by late afternoon, I can
imagine him, a pearl diver under all of this, pulling up
from his vast and still realm,

a clink. This came to me the other day as I was sprinkling dill
    into the borscht
because my brother's ring had been my grandfather's wedding
    ring
in post-revolutionary Russia and was most likely steamed by
    borscht —
the ruble almost worthless, typhus, drought, famine
and bandits

looting everything except a few potatoes for the borscht. I've
    read these things

in Uncle John's self-published translation of my great-
     grandfather's
sermons and papers, which includes historical notes as well as
     photos of murdered
Mennonite families (the rows of well-dressed
bodies in coffins)

which holds a certain cachet because the handwritten
pages were smuggled from Russia by my emigrating family, and
     because the book
was listed in the Acknowledgements in the hardcover edition of
     a best-selling,
award-winning Canadian historical novel. Still, it says
nothing

about Grandpa setting off hungry for Alexandrovsk that day in
     June 1921 in search
of rings, his stomach rumbling with the train over the arms
of the Dnieper (viewed on a map, these arms crookedly hold
the Island of Chortitza, over which his train also rumbled) into
the clang and soot

of the city where, as the sky was beginning to dim, his panic
     setting in and still
no rings, in a shop near Festival Square, in a glass case, in a bed
     of velvet, the pink gold —
pink for the copper that reduced the price — slid up his
     finger and would slide up the
finger of his wife, ride the Bruton (Mennonites filling an
     ex-military ship)
across

the Atlantic to find the surfaces of a new life: metal, wood, soil,
grain. Ties Grandpa spiked near Wymark, Saskatchewan no
     doubt heard
the ring, along with select Low German swearing, never used
     otherwise, in the heat
(stinking, sweating, unbearable) of 1924. Soil of Great Deer
too dry, too

poor, too utterly dusty, crumbled past the ring, spring after
  spring. Present
on the frosted night of my father's conception, also at spankings
  throughout
his boyhood, the ring is a glint from the pulpit in scripture, in
  prayer. My father,
doctor at his father's bedside, holds the hand, feels for the
  pulse, the ring smearing copper
across

the sky. He lets it go. Over the phone just now Dad informed me
  (casually
but with certainty) that Grandpa, daily in contact with tractor,
threshing machine, seeding machine, manure, butcher knives,
    pig
insides, cow insides, chicken wire, horse rope, etc., in fact
never wore

his wedding ring. This was confirmed by Uncle John who, in
  spite of having
just last night fallen asleep at the wheel causing him to roll his
  car and fracture
his TH8 backbone, in spite of his aging memory, was able to
  vouch with confidence
that Grandpa never wore the ring. So I'm left holding
nothing

except a clink against a steering wheel, my brother
heading north in love with the woman beside him, the radio on,
light rinsing the car so all you can do is squint
at highway line after line pulling you forward and you can't even
  see
the rear view.

Sestina for the Sweater

~ BARBARA NICKEL ~

One sleeve left. The rest has taken sixteen years,
begun in college for the boy who played
the violin. I was so young, just learning to cast
on, cast off, purl two, knit one. I'd lose
stitches, alone in the pew while he filled
the dark church with Sibelius. By 3 a.m., needles

forgotten, wool tangled on the floor, I'd knead
his shoulder for the secret of his gift. In a year
or two, I thought, we'd marry. But I wanted to fill
the sweater with another shape, and played
with his tears in wool, on wood. I chose another I knew I'd lose
even while he held out his hand, sun casting

brilliant shapes down the grave we leaned against. I cast
off guilt and stitches: a new armhole. Needles
of pine, King Lear, warm beer, his loose
way of walking I'd follow in and out of years
and off and on, gaps alone when I'd knit a ply
of my hair into the cuff. When I filled

my bag and left, the last time, grief filled
up my elbows and knees; I broke my wrist. The cast
kept me from knitting and playing
the violin. Too many mistakes. I stuck my needles
in a bag, safety-pinned the sweater from unravelling. That year
I found another I could never lose,

except we kept saying goodbye. But loss
I could count in days, by rows, measuring when next we'd fill
a week or two with love and stump-jumping. In the years
to come I'd stitch shoulder to neck, the cast
of our future green with the need
for acreages and children and the sweater that matched his eyes.
   I played

at this, outgrew it. One sleeve left. Sibelius playing
on the radio, I drive through rain, count the lost
strands of their lives, what it would take for my needles
to finish this into a whole. For whom? (Not my husband, he'll fill
my life. Besides, it wouldn't fit.) But to recast
myself into the sweater done, wool finally touching skin. (Years
   later, he tries it on, plays
with a cuff, finds my hair, refills his coffee, feels the loss, casts
me off, casts me on, sound of needles as we face the years —)

Moving

- BARBARA NICKEL -

Constant is the graveyard slanting up behind
the house in a wash of sunlight or in winds
that lash this coast where spruce bend,
lose branches, remain. Father had no words
at the airport but when we moved to the brim
of this country I saw his tears in the stars
splaying down the crevices of cliffs. From
Greenland icebergs travel to dissolve here;
their centuries' wisdom is salt I lick from my lip
in a fog. Constant is the moon's yellow eye
on water rushing from a campground pump
into a small, steel bowl I carry to our site.
With each step water sloshes out of bounds,
takes moonlight with it, finds strange ground.

Riding Freehand

- LARRY NIGHTINGALE -

". . . be you blithe and bonny, converting all
your sounds of woe . . ."

— SHAKESPEARE

Quick on
the heels of
summer-Sunday morning,
having had at all that
— the old preacher — the peppery
black rump of roast,
still hungry, up on our pedals and ram's-horn handlebars,
white shirts
billowing, cuffless and tieless now,
long necks forward, boys with
the hey nonny nonny good news.
All as if on one
bicycle, pumping
across the flats. Off across
the little prairie, far past the cattle call — the conscience's
shouts. On past
the creeping shadows
— the flag staff, the spire, the silo, and
the dry white bones. On,
on past that field of stones.
                              Is that us
gone wishing past? Heading out.
Cumulous. About to shine.
About to skim off clear, wearing nothing
— not even the silly milk-moustache.

Sunday afternoon in the green
pastures, all shall be buttercupped, daisy-chained and
bright . . .

Still pedalling hard
— how many life-longs later?
The long thread of the elders' sermon
still stitching
our sides, our big wishes
taking on a serious wobble.
Free-wheeling on, just out of the guilty reach,
out of guilty sight. Riding sun-blind,
sneezing at the shadows. Our souls (about to shine)
twist-and-shouting the freehand gospel.
Good news! Good news! Good news!

Cathedralesque

- LARRY NIGHTINGALE -

Cathedralesque, the beasts
under a sweeping black of rafters,

the dairy clanging, low cowbelled belfries,
and sudden rain — top of the shadow-roosts,
screech of the weathervane, and then the hail hammering,
a swishing, a shifting of hooves.

Above the loft a single small window
daylight-stained, burning monochrome,
filigreed cobwebs, dark dust,
and flitter of birds inside the shimmering,

shadows across a roughed hand
among saucer pools of last light,
shadows down the long loft ladder,
and in the blind pen
steaming breath, a white bull,
all stops pulled, a great organ piping,

like song and scripture —
all the rustling green ghosts of spring,
every silver shiver of straw
baled and barned into the Bible-blackness,
the book of days, the closing year,
whispering of summer's end and harvest.

Seven brothers in a row
relieving themselves, dreaming out
the great sliding cattle door,
out to where the tall pasture opens
and the birds rise up,
last notes from the vespers hymnal,
stanchions of grace, and each knows his place
in a world free and mapped in black
(so low the ragged night folds itself
into their prayers).

Barrel-burning

- LARRY NIGHTINGALE -

In the weeds, memory's
wandering a small-town maze — old wiggledy lanes.
It's late summer. It's Cemetery Avenue. They're barrel-burning
in a patchwork of old backyard gardens,
feeding time's clear amber fire. Elongated
flames are leaping up choking down prunings and grasses
— green armfuls. Raggedy, limp, and morning-dewy,
every leaf-shaped heart, every stalk and blade's weedy wonder.
Transforming in the profound furnace,
a great blueprint's redrawn.
Barrelled green and substantial — billowing out amber-white,
Eden's green work — elementally altered,
— abstracted — new matter
— in a low rolling cloud over the shining orchard, and soon
curling wisps out through the fields
— then clear haze in the far stands of corn.
And here's this pallid mound of powder — and white flakes of ash
on the good neighbour gravedigger's shovel and arm.

(Dear, isn't this where you came in, bounding
into my kitchen-cabana, sprigs of dill in loose braids,
you fresh from visiting round old Martha and Henry's
garden barrel next door,
straightway showing me a savoury way to fry up potatoes?)

And is this not how presence and experience feed and transform?
And how then memory abstracts? Nourishes? And flourishes?
Barrel-burning — a great blueprint redrawn
— living's green work to new matter.
Yes, we've some ashes up our sleeves.
And we're white smoke in time's orchard.
And in the garden furnace, in clear living memory,
we are this flame.

Parlour Song

- LARRY NIGHTINGALE -

So he rested here a while — his heart and hands,
rested as some sacred choir's long-time lost conductor

awake in this mystery of silence, this grace and strength
here in this long narrow room
a million autoharps rippling down
from the ghosts of old saint balladeers, from secret choir-lofts
from the Lord's high, holy, lonesome ruins.

Thanks for the visitation, brother.

Once there came other dark-clothed elders — itinerant singers
who napped here — a few winks in a casket at midday, after
a bowl of cold barley gruel with cream and a glass of black tea.

So now, the body stretched out full length, full ease.
Yet supple wrists and hands again somewhere crossing
— playing in a streaming sunbeam —

this joy is taller than the shadow

where brother John our mighty baritone now goes
striding, dancing with the fireflies and the bee swarm and
the chicory blue ghost of sister June . . . arm in arm, sweeping
   down
a long narrow room.
(Down that long narrow room, dance and sing!)

we sang the twilight hymn, prayed the mystery prayer,
walked the line, ringed the burning fire,
murmured the heart's high, holy murmur,
and together, with a simple turn, twirl and spin, black coat flaps,
shirttails, apron strings trailing, kicked off the lead-weight boots . . .

Nahanni River, Day 9

- MELANIE SIEBERT -

Chasm of Chills, Kraus' Hotsprings, Lafferty's Riffle
Basics — cold water, warm water, moving
water, suspended between rock and sky,

we are made mostly of water and all its moods
sweeping through the canyons.

Dryas shimmers in the throat of wind,
streamed of stars for days that don't go dark.

Here one stone carries the held breath of mountain,
a choir if we could hear that frequency.

Here we gather at the water
to remember the flow, the falling,

how to round rocks, how to cut
a course through ragged ranges.

Here we stop to bend the *coloured quills*
of praise and silence across our tongues.

"Dryas": a wildflower with poofy silvery plumes when it goes to seed, often
found growing on alluvial fans.

"coloured quills": refers to the porcupine quills that are chewed flat, dyed
bright colours and stitched as decoration on birchbark baskets by the Dene.

Tundra

- MELANIE SIEBERT -

1

Picture me: on the tundra,
the ground moist and sucking at my steps,
the rise so gentle.

At this pace I will walk
and never be out of sight.

2

I have dreamt of a land
this open, this light,
the sun revolving around my head.

3

In this land where you can hear for miles, the migration
of caribou is small thunder across my chest,
more trembling than sound.

Tracks, braille for the wind to read.

4

Barrenland —
on my knees I have found
swaths of arctic flowers.

5

Muskox lumber under the weight of ice-age
memory. The only animals
never to seek shelter from the cold
break into a run when my boots clatter over loose rock.

This is as close as I will get:
handfuls of qiviut, fine under-wool,
the warmest and softest,
caught in the tattered shrubs.

6

Wind —

                    ceaseless.

Dictating when I can and cannot travel.
Keeping me close to the ground.

7

I wake to find tracks outside my tent door:
the perfect silence of the animal
that has passed me by.

Memoir

- MELANIE SIEBERT -

(Found poem, from the writings of Abe Siebert)

1

The watermelons were ripe.
Mother helped unload the wagons,
carrying baskets full of melons
to cook into syrup.
That night she felt pains.

Thus, I was born,
December 1917, Southern Russia,
just north of the Sea of Azov.

2

Father and Grandpa were coming
through the door,
coming in
from the barn for breakfast.

I was three. A cannon shell struck
the large tree beside the house.
Father was one step inside,
Grandpa one step outside.

I am reminded of the scripture,
"There is one step
between me and death."

3

Behind our yard was a stream,
and beyond the stream an orchard.

We had apples, plums
and pears. It was a pleasure
to go there with cousin Lena
and sample all kinds of fruit.

Once I found a little blue egg,
which she fried for me.

4

We had to host and feed the armies
as they passed through, not knowing
if they were red or white.

We were Mennonites, pacifists.
When the soldiers made my father
dig up his father's grave,
they did not find guns.

5

In Riga, the harbour city of Latvia,
we were disinfected, our clothes baked.
For the first time I noticed electric lights.

I was seven when we crossed the Atlantic,
seasick, mother singing hymns in the dark,
green water through the portholes.

At sea, I played with a paper boat.
It could be flattened,
then reshaped back into a boat.

Desire

- MELANIE SIEBERT -

When I look up into
your god-strange and wanting
eyes, in that glance: the coming
rains, bare trees, fox-blaze.

When I look up —
the god-fox coming,
wanting as rain on trees, all
in your bare-eyed blaze.

And when the rain lets loose
wanting is forgotten,
the fox forgotten, the blazing
trees, the god-wanting trees

forgotten, when I look up,
                              raining
into your god-strange
and wanting eyes.

this traffic

- LEANNE BOSCHMAN -

my breath mingles with moist air;
countless droplets are one moment

      suspended — a shroud,
   then falling — a shower.
three ships in the harbour, loaded with grain
  or unfilled

thinking about how a woman could drift, too
freighted with a life-time of leavings,
   or soul-empty
for so long this traffic of rusting bodies
in the commerce of desolation, for so long
hull-punctured, waiting to be junked,
a woman can walk alone,
      disappear in the mist
  for   so long

West Coast Winter Solstice

- LEANNE BOSCHMAN -

Full cup of nightfall spills
all at once. Unclad
limbs of trees, wings of ravens, small
canopies of umbrellas immersed
in this glistening blackness.
How these evenings steep, so
many hours thicken,
a rich liquor of rain beads
from drain spouts, darkness
spiced with our sighs.

Morning will be late arriving, shadow-
drenched. Tonight in this
nocturnal world, untraversed
as the region behind our eyelids,
come, feast on black-
berries here ripening, taste
plums of impulse, draw in
deeply this bewitching breeze,
as we set our course for the far
                    edge of this longest night.

night rain

- LEANNE BOSCHMAN -

scent of it drifts
in from damp mountains
trees are ready   grass is ready   moss is ready   fish are ready
sidewalks ready   windowsills ready
then comes wind's sharp sigh   *wind's sigh*
pierces winter night   *pierces night*
sssssssssssssssssssssssssssssssssssiiiiiiiiiiiiiiiiiiiiiiiiiiiiiiiiiiiiiiiiiii
an open sky   sky opens and
down   falls   down   falls   down   falls
downfalls   downfalls   downfalls   downfalls
drops of glass   liquid trinkets   liquid glass   drops of trinkets
drops of blossoms   drops of blue   liquid blossoms   drops of blue
liquid silk   drops of turquoise   drops of silk   liquid turquoise
drops of darkness   liquid darkness   drops of moon   liquid rumours
liquid moans   drops of arrows   liquid bones   drops of sins
drops of cold   liquid atonement   drops of jabber   liquid chatter
drops of longing   liquid glances   liquid dancing
liquid swells   drops of petals   liquid murmurs
liquid notes
liquid stop   ping
notes stop   notes stop
notes   stop
notes
stop
o   p   o   p
o   p
o

Perdue

- LEANNE BOSCHMAN -

for Michael

The Capri Theatre in Perdue was not yet boarded up.
We ate popcorn, slurped pop out of waxy paper cups.
As dust motes swarmed in the projector's beam of light,
I stared at a young woman with funny short hair
bounding over mountaintops, singing.
We knew mountains only in pictures and ran up
piles of gravel, over tractor tires, to *Do, Re, Mi.*

Michael lay in his room, blinds pulled on hot days;
Mom said he had brain fever, so there was no one to be Friedrich.
Then the others had mumps; Mom said leave them to rest.
Their pale moon-faces at the window, they all watched as I ran
between clothes flapping on the line, leapt through a small
opening in the caragana hedge, tumbled out the other side.

So many hours I spent searching for those children.
Brother, you were lost so often — three hours in the back
of an old pickup before I found you — Mom crying
where can he be?
All those evenings we spent playing rescue. Saving you from fire
wasn't easy, but the flames parted if I was brave.
In the light of the hospital room it was harder —
even to stand still.

So many years later I still dream that they all follow
behind me in a row, and I am Maria again
teaching the children to sing.

You are Here

- LEANNE BOSCHMAN -

1) you are here.
   where you stumble through burnt pastures
   the moon a luminescent bruise on the horizon

2) you are here.
   where you pronounce each letter of your longing
   always a foreign tongue sounded on the wind

3) you are here.
   where you crack open the black secret of night
   watch the shells fall at your white feet

4) you are here.
   where you consume the boundaries of your faith
   shed your skin as an offering
   before you have grown a new one

Moment 3

- ELSIE K. NEUFELD -

You can feel it inside when you wake. A faint shift
in each cell like a runnel of air your skin knows
is there but can't name. Bones unsettled, it's that deep
in your marrow. Dawn later each morning, birds quiet
evenings sooner and long. What's worse, early or late?

Last night you closed all the windows. Watched
the sun set from inside. The far purpled mountains
and clotted pink skyline merged after dark. Moths
ticking the luminous panes, their white wings on glass
like a frayed marmalade label. Everything's drawn

to what's absent. The light all night left on. These
days you look at the garden less often. The dirt under
dropped blossoms baked hard. A lament in each
colourless spot. You tell yourself nothing
is barren though it seems otherwise. What's gone

shows up elsewhere. Those raised blue veins
on hands that resemble your mother's. Thin stripes
of gill-silver tracks on buttocks and belly. Benign
birthmarks. The skin is a calendar-clock, the imprint
of hours. This is the time you wished for, wanted

never to come. The world in fall as a low flame ignited
again and again till it's gone. The switch always
too sudden! You know this for certain when you start
talking to mirrors. A stranger inside remembering you
to those black and white photos, and your son's

question about colour on earth: *when did it start?*
Now, when you turn to the window you see fewer
singular hues. The shift within named as you imagine
slender white roots curled underground into one.
A dead fly on the hem of the curtain.

On Looking inside a (Blue-Clip) Campanula

- ELSIE K. NEUFELD -

You could get lost in that crawling
violet flower   dirt hidden below and stars
wandering the curved edge of bed in the
garden   thumb-long blossoms opening wide
on leaves stippled with sighs   their thin stamens
gossamer-pronged and glistening   want
the light touch of a lover   the sun rising
and falling   a round word whispered aloud
is love nothing more
than a fleeting tongued hollow?
the thread-slender flesh deep inside quivered
even the hummingbird quick to move on.

Wedding Rings

- ELSIE K. NEUFELD -

There, in a box, under a quilted white cotton
they couple. Too small now for a finger
swollen with time. The quiet dark shared

with torn hose, a lace slip, the broken
black strap of a watch. Things you meant
to get rid of. Some things are like that:

an earring, loose pearls. Your ill-fitting
bands, golden beginnings and
endings. Once you considered a friend's

advice to melt the two rings into one.
Old ones made new, the diamond on top
cleaned and polished. A fresh clasp.

At first you disguised its absence. Left
hand covered with right. Sooner or later it's all
common. Nothing's exempt. The marital

finger, that honest bare skin. Questions
and answers: Yes, yes. I do. Have rings
safe in a box   at home.

Weisst Du Wieviel?

- ELSIE K. NEUFELD -

Mosquitoes hum as you sing the child's song of stars
and clouds. Ponder their numbers, how God knows each one
by name   counts even the hairs on your head — the fallen
the new ones growing.

You sing the words in German as you sit alone. A black
cat at your feet, head turned on its side in your empty
shoe   its dark sole a resting place that remembers your foot
and Jacob's stone pillow (Jacob, the hairiest).

It's an old story. Clouds parted and heaven split open
to loose a long ladder   rungs of light within easy reach
of a dreamer who wrestled fiery angels down. You
believe this is true, sing knowing the song's questions

will end. Recall a hard church pew, hands splayed
on its cold wooden edge to pillow your shivering legs.
Children packed in front rows like lyrics, you tried
to sit quiet. A choir before you, fathers and mothers

watching your back, and suspended above, a crowd
of young deaf-mutes. A far cloud of witnesses. Souls
of your dead humming along with *Weisst du, wieviel
Sternlein stehen . . . weithin über alle Welt . . .* Voices

breaking into a four-part song about clouds in the sky
fish in the sea and a God who knows all: *Gott der Herr
hat sie gezählet, dass ihm auch nicht eines fehlet . . .*
Oh, how you loved the world when you sang of stars

and nights filled with the pin pricks of mosquitoes
drinking your blood! Their high whine slapped silent
on blossoming welts. Wings, stinger and limbs in your palm
a black-and-red blemish. Heaven's needle-eye long

as the cat's yawn and arched back when it lifts off
your shoe and moves on. Fur against skin as it sweeps past
like those stars and clouds you imagined
God counting.

Weisst Du Wieviel: Can you count the number?

Wishbones

- ELSIE K. NEUFELD -

for John

birds singing the light and this morning is filled with sharp
    edges   spent the last
hour exhuming my night-long musings   don't think I've ever
    considered bones
like that   all those questions in the God poem last night took
    me back to brother
& me playing tug-of-war, not with a rope, with a hen's wishbone.
    Hands latched

on spurred ends, brother's loud *GO!* the finger-long V-bone see-
    sawed between
us   up-down and up until CRACK!   the break jagged and one
    of us sing-saying
ha ha. I'm going to live long-er than you-oo! The winner's hooded
    half swished
through the air like that staff Jesus carried to snag strayed lambs
    trapped

in brambles   but who knows? could be a question mark too or
    worse   I mean
the victor's long half of wishbone   the short portion a shard in
    the hand a mark
in the palm   my carnivorous soul gnawing old bones and go
    ahead chew
if that's what it takes to find him   do you believe the dead leave
    the grave and

if so how are they found and where do they go? I mean all that
blood his spine
neck & skull broken   it took days to identify my brother   his
lovely young face
erased in the fire   brows nose and mouth gone gone   only
teeth in a hole   bones
to confirm *yes . . .   yes . . .   positively*

it *is* him

he *is* dead

knees thighs and legs crushed — head-on — feet spared   that's
all we saw
could touch in the casket   those gap-tooth toes a family trait
his running
shoes poised in the car like he was coming back   perhaps I
should have
taken them home flung them tied on a wire   proof he was dead
or a sign

he'd return cause he did   he came back   not flesh and bone
but you know
how that goes how the longer they're gone the closer our dead
travel
could be like you say in a cat or a hawk on a cedar's thin bough or
a wishbone.

What's Memory?

~ ELSIE K. NEUFELD ~

Sometimes I wonder what the living
remember last and the dead first ponder

father bent to the west to the sundown
his heart beating lines in a box and the cuff
round his arm like those sleeve-bands he wore
as a pallbearer   half of him frozen already
and it's not even noon   his family on guard
whispering *stay* though they're wishing he'd go
go to where his dead lie in wait
his father and mother   son   five brothers and

friends what's memory but a key to the gates
of heaven or a magnet to draw the dead
back to life and the dying towards death
it's so hard to let go and still harder
to travel alone to a home long forgotten
or believe in one's end as beginning
his hands stiff as spent flowers

Who can define alpha omega or say
whether the hands over there are as warm
or if he remembers the feel of flesh
over bones or a pulse   that last rasping

The Whole Steppe before the Fall

- ELSIE K. NEUFELD -

My mother at twelve sits in the shade of an acacia
its wide bole worn as the Ukrainian steppe behind
the rich land bearing far less than this tree its branches
bent low and seed dropped in her apron   meals

every day now water and bones boiled over
and over for soup. Knives and forks long ago hidden
my mother pretending her hunger is gone, and afterwards
eating more blossoms. Tongue against teeth like plough

turning fields under a star-and-sickle flagged sky and she
every day wanting more. Lips chapped, her people
and land bled by famine and she not yet a woman.
Bloated, like the roots of the tree and hungry, so

hungry, my mother at twelve ponders the limbs'
rhythmic squeak and cracked bark then remembers
her father. A loud knock after dark, his hand
in her hair as he told her a story of manna

falling to earth, and in its aftermath, quail.
His last whispered words a prayer in her ear
Let none of them starve.

My mother at twelve, her tongue swollen
and teeth filled with grit, swallows again
and again   a husk caught
in her throat.

Yesterday's Kill

- ELSIE K. NEUFELD -

Grey weather drifting back to pigs on the farm
flat snouts into warm mash. Father walking
the fog like a ghost wading dark water. Arm pressing rifle
across his chest, his fist in a pocket, steps measured
to the barn. Door opened with a kick, the wind
slamming it shut. A bullet slipped into his palm.

It's a webbed world. Dew pearled on each thread
and a black fly buzzing
stuck on the long legs of yesterday's kill.
No spider.

In summer my brothers and I fed the pigs
chickweed and yellow squash. Leaves scratched
our fingers and Mother warning *Passt auf!* The butcher
knife sharpened with Dad's spit on a whetstone
and harvest disguised beneath vines like a prowler.
Stems prickly and skins opening hard to a tumble
of pulp. Time dragging, the cut squash piled higher.

Pigs in the barn, without thought.
Dad's trigger finger pulled back, a dark hole
glistening the hairy white hide.
The pig with one shot to its forehead toppled
onto its side, legs twitching, blade stuck
in femoral artery the red smile spread wide.

My father denied shooting enemy soldiers.
Laughed when I asked *did you kill any?*
He grinned when he said *helmet . . . hung
on a stick . . . my head to the ground.* Dirt
glittered wet with piss blood and water.

In prison he slept in the middle. Captives
too close to the edge of the fenced yard
were shot for moving an arm.

A fire at dawn, pigs skinned and hung
on a rod. Smoke and steam off a cauldron,
a hand stirring salt into sausage. Father's
head bowed. Fog on the ground.

November Snow

- ELSIE K. NEUFELD -

"I can scarcely wait for tomorrow.
When a new life begins for me,
as it does each day."

— STANLEY KUNITZ, "The Round"

Tonight, snow lanterned the garden's last pink anemone
and poppy. The slim yew, rose bush and helleborus held
in its spell. Stalks, leaves, buds sculpted anew, the dark
field illumined by thousand-tongued chandeliers. Raised
beds and meadow, forest and ceiling of air. Heaven tethered
to earth in flashes of weather fragile as moth wings & bones.
Kunitz saw dawn's shell-pink light fade on a flower. I saw

the night, the dead come to life. Snow crafting bare limbs
into crooked white fingers and hands the skin a thick dust
feathering cracks into nests. The oak a perch for ghost-flocks
of birds long ago lulled into a cold sleep, the cloaked plant-rot
below dreaming in ivory pillars and roof. I wanted more. So,
at midnight I flung the door open & entered the quiet design.
Ah, yes! *I can scarcely wait for tomorrow.*

Baltimore Oriole

- K. LOUISE VINCENT -

At thirteen my friends and I roamed
the streets like troubadours. At night
we sang like maniacs and howled
for all we were worth. At fourteen
we seared our lungs hot-knifing hash
in abandoned box-cars. Later, we huddled
at the corner of Szcoloski's garage, smoked
stolen Export A's, unfiltered. It was
a surprise the evening your blue Pontiac
inched closer, your face in the window.
The slightest smile when you said,
each one of you, get in the car, now.

We did and a silence drove us
until you pulled over
on an old logging road. We sat expecting
our crimes to be listed, our secrets laid
open. But you simply whispered, *listen.*
We waited, five disoriented teenagers
beside the gentle green of trees. We heard
one short note, then four long ones
delivering day to night, a passage of time
punctuated with precision of prayer.
It was the first time I thought clearly
about love, the first time I felt the nearness
of peace. *That,* you said,
is a Baltimore oriole.

I Find all Devotion Difficult

- K. LOUISE VINCENT -

these days. The details I love
have been painted over, white-washed.
My mind has pulled down an empty
screen, my heart has shut
the damper shut. *The works of all
the visionaries have walked away.*

Seaweed glows black on the garden beds.
Silent graves of bulbs and roots
relate more now to the stars and night.
During the day, shadow is blue
light is the way we move inside
the shadow, boreal and burning —

like Kepler when he worked faithfully
in the dark, clear with what he loved.
When he felt the moonlight warm on his hands
he thought someone was breathing behind him.
From a distance, devotion seems difficult.
Up close, I see the heart of the world
is broken; it is winter and there is war.

Walking the Trapline

- K. LOUISE VINCENT -

You pace the apartment where you live
now. Having relinquished everything with roots,
earth and water. Your boat, garden,
home and phone number of forty-two years.
A man who knows where the prairie melts
into precambrian shield, who translated
thousands of bush trails, who listened
to every bird that sang within
his distance. Today the size of this space is so small
it can be held in one glance.
Walking the trapline we call it
when you circle the kitchen and living room
as though invoking in each careful step
every animal you touched.

How to alleviate an agitation vast and long
as a river you fished? Today there are no fish
swimming in your veins. Today the chemicals
injected to outrun the cancer take
three lines to write.

We sit together and watch television. In Ethiopia
people are forced to climb to the top of trees
and hang on. The last bit of green
imprinted in their palms before the brown sludge
sweeps them away.

I return later after my first walk for years
in Manitoba bush. I am more myself
my hands full of pussy willows. Their soft bodies,
embryos of forgotten animals whose existence
we never doubted. All the years in my childhood
we placed them dry in a vase
but this Spring you add water so they can keep
growing, you say.

Open Sky

- K. LOUISE VINCENT -

We lie on your bed, side by side
reading. Your body each day
revealing its skeleton, sharper now
and your skin, thinner.
We are peaceful, sometimes completely
content. You reading Louis L'Amour, me
John Berger describing the unspoken joy
of two solitary old men sharing a meal
then weeping with the wine.
You said, *well it's only westerns now*
with the morphine it has to be
that simple. We adjust your pillows,
turn pages, each in a story
of land and dislocation, of time
when everyone slept under the open sky,
wept secretly in the sweet air.

When the Dark Work Started

- K. LOUISE VINCENT -

I listen in the kitchen mesmerized
by my mother and her sisters, ten women speaking
French, my aunties with names that sound like catechism.
Conversation bursts like multiplication,
two statements give rise to four, four to sixteen,
an exponential dialect erupting from cigarettes, coffee, canasta.
Someone slaps a wildcard down. They talk louder now,
sounds surge until the room ruptures with names
of husbands and children, profanities and laughter.
They kiss me, each one as they leave.
French words fly for hours through the air.

My father and his brother sit in armchairs
in the living room speaking German,
the tone of their voices what I expect
in a church, reinforcing my belief
Low German meant not talking loud.
Their conversation has a slurred cadence,
a linearity, I know when they begin
and end. There are silences. Sometimes
they laugh in their slow way then pause.
I am unaware they speak of private lives
that subdue rather than reveal.

As a child I was astounded
and aroused by language I didn't understand.
I became a word thief, a pirate, my body
full of hijacked lyrics and laments.
Words settled in my bones,
mystery desired to speak
the sweet sorrow and wild authority
of mother tongue.
It was in that duplex on Pine Street
the dark work started.

a little mennonite goes a long way

- ROBERT MARTENS -

we have nigh pleasured ourselves to death,
sing the children. orgasm is immortal,
say the ads. so if you ask me,
drowning as we are in the
syrup of our lusts, everyone could use a
little mennonite at their side. dressed
in black. hollow-eyed and tight-lipped.
gloom pressing like anvils on his shoulders.
recondite in homilies of grief. and

(1) if things feel just fine and brand new
(2) if everything is going a bit
too well (3) if you have no regrets (4) if
someone seems to have all the answers
(5) if the latest toy is a lot of fun
(6) if you're interviewed on tv and the interviewer
smiles a lot (7) if you win an award
(8) if there are brand new plans for reform (9) if the
poor are well cared for and (10) everyone is
free (11) if you're having a good time
(12) if the world is at peace (13) if morning
seems just right (14) if the house
is neat and clean (15) if you haven't
lost anything lately — the little mennonite

will studiously clear his throat, and tell you

(1) this world is old and broken-down (2) it's
headed for collapse (3) and you're responsible
(4) there are no answers (5) pleasure is the
devil's invitation to hell (6) killers like to
smile (7) and hand out awards just before they
murder you (8) this world can't be fixed
(9) the poor are with us always (10) freedom
(11) contentment (12) and peace are
illusions (13) eternal evening is just around
the corner (14) when we shall all be caught
unprepared and (15) everything will be lost.

all this advice could spoil your evening. but
don't resent it, the little mennonite has your
best interests at heart, he only wants to prepare you
for the worst, which always happens. so
sit down with him, share some zwieback and borscht.
you know, he says, turning to you gravely,
kindly, *this could be our last meal.*

and the lord said,
i will destroy man. . .

- ROBERT MARTENS -

rusty rainbow tacked to mountain peaks.
plodding parade to an ark
at the end of time. he imagines
he must be noah, resurrected from
the deep blue bottom of an eon's wrath.
is someone watching? herding these
animals into a rickety slaughterhouse,
merciful god, dumb beasts. he raises

his arm like a thunderbolt. *if only
i could free you,* he says, and they
trudge to their deaths, voices frail
as a cracked violin, romantic, forgiving . . .
and it begins to rain. two by two,
down the rift of the valley where
the freeway begins. lions purring and
meek. wolves with their heads bowed.
elephants bearing wounded serpents.
epiphany of rising rivers, snort and
grunt, bellow and bleat, the
love of this lucid hour. *i could
turn and live with you,* he says. as
traffic slows to rush, as men sell ideas
to the next day, auction off
the last, humble beast. oh

speechlessness of fur and hoof, release
we can't face, miracle of haunches
turned against the rain.
we were here, too, if we could
only remember. carried off
by floods of innocence.

visions of rapture

- ROBERT MARTENS -

he was hiding behind the curtain, or maybe
under that boulder, he was veiled in the
phrases that dripped like sulphur from
the preacher's tongue. at any moment he might
leap out, holler BOO! scare the hell out of you.
the lord, they said, would return exactly when
you least expect it, when you're imagining sex
with your neighbour, perhaps, or when your
wicked nerves twitch back a coin from the
sunday morning plate, that could be the time —
and while the rest of them are shouting amens
atop sunbeams and chortling at the ones left
behind — *your* destiny is forever made.
you hadn't submitted to the lord's forgiveness.
go ahead, fall on your knees, it's too late,
satan's already blistering your butt with his
favourite pitchfork, and high-pitched hymn-singing
isn't going to fool him. we kids were
spooked into heaven. again and again.
walked down the church aisle, heads bowed,
down, down into contrition, to where
the evangelist waited, solid as the altar
of abraham, one foot already in paradise,
pray, the lord is merciful to humble children.

behold, i show you a mystery, we shall
not all sleep, but be raised incorruptible,
in the twinkling of an eye. our mennonite village
slumbered uneasily. waited, hoped for an end.
we shall not bear arms, the ministers said,

god will avenge his own. and what
choice did they have? stalin had proved the
devil right, only the rich are stupid enough
to believe in justice. so we scrubbed off
the manure smell, greased down our hair,
bribed the lord with a buck and a prayer,
and don't drowse during the sermon or the
floorboards may crack open under your feet.
the lord's vengeance is the faithful servant's
best hope. then there was the man, the story
is told, took his trumpet to the church rafters,
blew it sweet and clean, shocked the folk below
into beautiful dreams, the lord has come.
later, they walked home together,
laughed it off in low german,
but believing.
believing. refugees
from heaven.

statement of assets

- ROBERT MARTENS -

1

i can't offer you much.

(my personal fortune) this
          is what i've got:

a medium house in a medium town a medium heart neither
here nor there but singed on a rare winter morning by sparks
of heaven and drear archaic in medium time on the proper
ice-ponds of hell

a job that chews at the foundations of my illusions wage too
great for a subverted poet bank accounts of silicon and a
driveway through the motherboard of my brain and uploaded
at the sign-in sheet a manager who unpages codes of contract
and forcible respect

an affliction diagnosed benign the fevers of books that built a
stockade that choked in the addicted flames of polite barbarian
hordes and the predictable music of a digital score transcribed
into daily routine and plunder and the things that will be

most modest apparel bargained from the garage sales of mother
corp and chosen with scruple not to offend not to take offence
and the fears of a farmkid in town blinded by the light ulcerated
by the city dividing city proliferating into city of infinite rebirth
unbuddhist into family of none

an honest ability to turn away tolerate the errors of neighbours foibles of friends murders by the powerful in their armour of fashion and an evening song and smile for the dying children of other planets and breakfast with strong coffee before this time vanishes into goodnight

and brief mornings of happiness minefields of the soul and all this can't be spoken and this poem shouldn't be read and this present stillness crippled hand shaken hope early sunshine dark ivy twining blue trunk of sky no more only this

that's all i can offer

to my many enemies

2

    in the morning mail
        a letter marked

            OCCUPANT

last will and legacy
    of someone
        you never knew
rely on the stranger

        when i

          (interrupted)
peered out the front window, suspicious   that he might
   come calling

          are you looking for

  anything in particular?

          can i help you?

  i
've never lived here, but
  the stranger has.
i don't wake up in the same bed,
  the stranger does.

i
have no name.
the stranger is
many names, seasons, times. once
he was a gunslinger, mad
    outlaw
packing his sins on his hip,
lost and punished kid
lazing down the southern river of dreams
                (see atlas appendix): but

he's stranger than all that. and he's

sitting at your table.

trust him.
he's travelled far, he's
never left home, he'll
lend you his riches, he hasn't got a
dime, he's no one, he's
more than you are,
no friends, no enemies,
no losses, no luck.

and he
        trusts me.
                i will tell you
his sacred lies.

eulogy

- ROBERT MARTENS -

your paper clip grin can't
      protect you. THEY'RE
NOT AS FRIENDLY AS YOU THINK.
haven't you noticed? — this is a
funeral that's ploughing our green valley,
      and the spring rains
are washing away our sins.
               over there —
in the corner, with her eyes
      burning through scripture —
that's one of them. she's
        passed on, but hey —
        she's not stupid, she
hasn't forgotten a thing. wait for it
      now — the little pause between
clichés — look, there, next to the entrance,
standing proud, idle, and free,
      clean in bone & blood, they're
        watching you and —
        the dead
        are losing patience,
   fidgeting past
heaven hell eternity
        and you
        trying to save their souls
when every last illusion was scattered
      seed to grave —   but

they're not angry.   (yet)   just
bored with you, really, they think
    you're in bad taste.
    friend.   brother.   don't be uneasy.
    let's rest in peace.

mittagschlaf

- ROBERT MARTENS -

i don't write poetry
on sunday afternoon. i don't
pray over our valley of sorrows
on sunday afternoon.
i don't plough fields, or
build barns, or
milk cows on
sunday afternoon. this
was taught by old
mothers and fathers:
mennonites
do not
on sunday afternoon.
nothing matters
on sunday afternoon. the
week so long,
centuries of grief,
a dark and homeless people
and loved ones taken, but
not
on sunday afternoon.
time for rest.
mittagschlaf: afternoon sleep
like a gentle wrestler,
you stagger to the nearest
couch, your shoes thud
on the floor, your
breathing warm and deep

as furrowed earth,
and tired bones nearly
dead with pleasure.

i write these words
on the anxious blank page
of the weekday. it's
raining hard, but i avoid
the comfort of the fire,
drink strong coffee, i
need to stay awake.
work hard, sunday afternoon
is close at hand. i don't
download dirty tricks
on sunday afternoon, or
pace the syringe streets,
or slip down the spine of the freeway.
i don't read poetry
on sunday afternoon,
the poem is complete.
on the seventh day
he slept. in his
dreaming soul, it is always
sunday afternoon,
he may never awake, he
shifts in his sleep,
a voice reaches out and
soothes his tangled hair,
peace, little ones,
the days of work
are nearly done.

us walking, the dog

- MELODY GOETZ -

& yesterday, the way the world was a poem around us waving
while you spilled your guts, your rage that said over & over
the world has betrayed me — everything has betrayed me, & while the
rain came down steady, pelting into our jackets & I prayed
for the right things to happen, I saw a flicker of movement in
the corner of my eye (like a poem, I thought, a soft shadowy
motion), then it was born into our world — your angel became
a black dog old as my childhood — friendly & shy, just a little.
& while we walked along the hard line of your anger, the dog
trotted a joyous dotted line — in one driveway & up another,
down the road & back to us for a meeting. the cars kept coming
& he didn't care — he would wait in the centre of the road for
them to come — headlights flaring in the dark, a sudden swerve
at the end when they saw his eyes. I grabbed his collar then,
pulled him with me to the side of the road, & when the car had
passed I released him into the night again, his joy re-surfacing as
easily as a fish into the rain. & me smiling, even chuckling at him,
remembering that moment when he emerged into the world

beside us like a shadow growing skin & bones, & a dog's delight.
& while you railed & pained against things already past & fading
into age, the wind picked up, & for a moment the world stopped
when you did, looking at some old garden hose by the curb
running full tilt, when you said with the first note of longing,
of release — *look at all that clean water*, & stood for a moment
with your boots in the stream

by any other name

- MELODY GOETZ -

it's happened to him twice now. once, cleaning the sanctuary,
alone on a Tuesday morning; the light weak, streaming
through narrow openings in the blinds, dust shimmering
& moving in the sun. he was bending over the table of the
Eucharist, *In Remembrance of Me* carved on it in wood hard &
deep; he was dusting the letters, & he says it was then that the
spirit pushed him. he did not fall over, he kept his balance,
but in the swiftness of his surprise, he caught the corner of the
table on his leg, & *o shit*, hopping about the sanctuary, blood
seeping & staining his pantleg; he was surprised & somewhat
irritated that the spirit had pushed him.

then it was Saturday night, a while past the first time; he had
just finished photocopying the Sunday morning bulletin & he
needed rest, he needed quiet; he went into the sanctuary to
be away from the noise of the streets & the drunks coming by
from the hotel next door & his wife pursing angry lips for
every second he was not home with the kids. he turned the
lights off & closed the door; he sat on the waterstained rug in
the sanctuary & rested his head back against the wall & needed
to hear nothing but the stillness of God & the half darkness.
& he was not thinking of miracles, or noble holy thoughts, no,
he thought of nothing but the end of the day & the still air in
his ears, in the room, his hands lying on the hard brown fibres
of the rug. then it caught his eye, just the corner of his eye, the
hem of a garment that was sweeping & floating, & then the spirit
sashayed near him, preening, glittering, then he saw nothing
but the dust colour of the wall & air, then a glimpse of her foot,
then he was not sure it was feet but maybe feathers, pinions, &
now he was angry, she disturbing him, she always there when he

was trying to get done, & he bounded to his feet, to where he
had seen the last flash of white, of colour, & she moved faster
faster while he, suddenly almost weightless with rage pursued
her — *who are you, damn it,* & his heavy chain of keys, ring of keys
ringing suddenly like chimes at his waist & he tore them from
his belt loop, flashing gold like trumpet in the sun as he threw
them at her, at nothing really — they landed hard against the
front wall, leaving a noticeable dent near the pulpit & slithered,
jingling metal to a heap on the floor.

he told me this outside after supper, the brown sparrows
fluttering, light-ridden on the roof.

bus ride

- MELODY GOETZ -

the woman across the aisle is trying not to cry, her blonde hair
brittle, lips smudged, eyes lined with black

white cat hairs cling to her black wool skirt; her eyes are full &
red with water. the bus groans to a halt, lets on a load of children,
laughing, shoving, chattering. between two of them, like looking
   through
the crotch of a tree, her face is framed — harsh & raw eyes &
   grief

the kids troop off the bus, leave us again in silence; the woman
   begins
to wail, & everything becomes a prop — the hotel, the stores
   outside,
the sky — the windows of the bus shudder & threaten to
   crumple,
disappear in a puff of dust; the street rolls up
like an old newspaper, the bus sinks into
nothing, & we are left
sitting, bodies arranged in rows —
watching our hands turn transparent,
& the world fill with this
woman, & her
red lipstick
Grief

Deen's Diner

- MELODY GOETZ -

1

the waitress with dyed hair and dark under her eyes sits at a table
takes a napkin and places upon it a spoon, a fork, a knife,
rolls it all up like a sausage in a pancake — then another napkin,
a spoon, a fork a knife, a napkin spoon
fork knifea napkinspoonforkknife, at indiscriminate
intervals, she takes a puff from her cigarette,
or a sip of coffee from an old
white mug

2

the newspaper in the garbage pail by the door, red vinyl
chairs and chrome, front window flashing
a late sun

Watermark

- MELODY GOETZ -

I missed your
step on the stairs,
didn't hear you leave.
I have to stop

trying, I am not a vessel —
you slipping through
my fingers like water.
it is not possible

to possess — not by words,
not by promises, not by hard
moulded gold rings,
not by deeds & print,
not by poems.
I am left with this

filling & emptying, water levels
measured by deposits on rocks,
the fitful night cries of a loon.
I cannot
keep you,
you are water   around
& with me, you are not
me, I am my only possession,
and even this
is circling, & does not hold

Strawberries

- LYNDA GRACE PHILIPPSEN -

she is just seven
sitting in the midday sun selling strawberries
her sweetness offered in paper baskets
promise of red juice heaped high and round

a man stops
yes I would like your strawberries
two baskets please
how much?

she cannot calculate the price
she is just seven
here
he gives her ten crisp dollars

what to do now?
she has no float
she cannot make change
she is just seven

someone told her she could sell strawberries
and made her believe it too
nobody mentioned change
nobody tallied the price
she doesn't know what it costs
she is just seven

what misguided notion put her
at the roadside in the midday sun
with her fragile offering
not knowing how much she would have to give back?

A Poem for My Father Whom I Kiss on the Mouth

- LYNDA GRACE PHILIPPSEN -

we lay the soaker hoses in spring
softly, speaking little
my father and I wend and wind
dip and twist through the garden

the hoses follow his hands and always lie flat to the ground
my father understands this — I do not
when I try they resist and I must weigh them down with stones

we dance through the garden joined by black hose we
press under foliage close to the ground
all summer roots drink in darkness
send new shoots to light

in fall we lift the hoses
lay them in long lines on the lawn
father's hand guides them onto the reel
coiled against winter tight and close

Inside

- AL REMPEL -

inside the forest, striped with shadows
laid thick on the moss-filled floor
we are silent for a while, and stare

we have pushed in from outside
through rose-hipped and prickled bushes
willow in the wet spots, and devil's club
rising in a broad-leafed canopy above us
we have slid down ravines and bit our lips
at rock-jarred shins, then scrambled up
moss has given way beneath our fingers
stained and smelling like the fresh mountain soil
we have noted the changes and kept track
of the hints of coming pine-bough scents
here the willow leaves off, here the alder
has fought the towering spruce — and lost

now we stop and breathe easy
feast a little on red-bright drops of cranberries
then find a moss-capped stump
sit and look back at the way we came
noting first the sweaty webs on our faces
then the slant of light in the trees,
and the time it spells
then nothing, but the slow breathing
that is the forest, and everything in it

Tilt

- AL REMPEL -

we slid to the north, hanging
on one long cedar bough
the mountain soil jammed up
under shoelaces, tongues and
down our socks, and the smell
of stinging nettle at our noses

we slid to the north, over
and over, didn't realize
its pull, the thin green line
of northern lights one night
driving back from Seattle

we slid to the north and here
I am caught by all of it
and in the summer, the arctic light
glows like an eye, its lid not quite
closed, and I'm dizzy with earth's tilt

Spine

- AL REMPEL -

what was I supposed to say
stumbling over the flat above
our campsite in the starry dark
when you asked if I believed
in astrology — planets lining
up with constellations, and the fact
that we were planting here together

all I knew then were the trees
and the stabbing pain as they went
into the ground, planting ravines
sliding over devil's club and you
calling to the crows one afternoon
until your voice went hoarse
those spruce plugs gone bare-root,
fist-sized, dug lines into my waist

how was I supposed to know
what pain would be in my back
ten years later, or how much
I wanted my vertebrae to line up
like all your planets and stars
bone on bone clicking into place
and breathing my fate with a sigh

In Reverse

- AL REMPEL -

work backwards from a long smoke
from the clouded swirl into the bowl
gathered up in flame first, then unlit
tobacco, the air sucked clean down
the pipe, the slow exhale in reverse
the lips pursed and the teeth clamped
cheeks slacken, the tongue curious and moist
and finally, the pipe laid in a box

don't you wish you could pack up
the universe this way, tidy the galaxies
and stuff the dark matter into a pouch?
never worry about fires again? take the way
things are between you and me, can't we
just unwind the strands of smoke
before it churns to haze? I bet

we'd all be jamming our boxes
and pouches full, filling the shelves
without bothering even to label things
and whistling some god-awful tune
while we wash our hands afterwards

This Summer

- AL REMPEL -

inside out   every afternoon
thunder rolls   the cataract sky
clouds over   and leaves
a hazy pool   like a warm bath
you want to slip into   no need
to think   the ravens taken to the trees
make copper-pipe noises   somewhere behind
the walls   as if the entire works
elbows and legs   the plumber
calls them   spilling out
with the water   gurgles and glooks
and knocks   the ripple
of electrified air   the hollow boom
all wet and dripping   through
leaves   onto a black shock
of feathers   turned

In the Age of Megastructures

- JEFF DERKSEN -

Often I am pressured
to return to Khrushchev
the cold moments
of the model kitchen, the shoe removed
in the General Assembly
a time permeated (perma-frosted) with the optimism
of modular stackable habitable
concrete "space frames
with plug-in units"

Someone like You

- JEFF DERKSEN -

Dear Capitalism, please
give me a reason
to believe. And then off I go
on the technoscape
not high above but
with pulsing pockets and sopping
opportunities in public space!
This nation is fine if only
it could be in the present
like Peter Sellers (not the "Indian"
Peter Sellers): sorry start again:
the movement from the past to the present
was hard, but I got to keep
my car to handle the curly roads
of the ethnoscape: sorry start again:
you are your mode
of production surfing the long waves
of capitalism in a tube
and you lose your bikini top
and only Elvis will
give it back and the small *e*
Levis of your youth *are* your retirement
fund. The summary then:
we are flying your dad in
for a consultation because we
all of us are very disappointed
in your rate at closing today
so borrow my Metrocard and go to

the Freud Museum daily followed
by a coffee in the café
where Lukács read through the cold
organizing winters and forget that form is never more
than a reflection of the relations
of production. As an organizing principle
I'm inept

Sly Consumption Side Sentence

- JEFF DERKSEN -

Dear neoliberalism, I
just want to thank you
for letting me
be a mobile
self-reflexive
commodity with agency
putting no pressure
on former state structures
anew, again
till you use me up
consumption side
just like you did
production side with Dad
add an *e*, dead

Everybody's Happy Nowadays

- JEFF DERKSEN -

I have lived my life
as if in a lament
as if cemented in
a file folder
of another's devising
or vision of the future
much like the now
I can't quite own
To be alone, transnationally
and more
than a little queasy
is the chorus
after the burning red-hot
power cords

Space Replaced (over Time)

- JEFF DERKSEN -

for Vancouver

A time when spaces
opened as voices
and seeing yourself meant
handles dealt with real
modernist unmaskings of power
using glass passively
exaggerated places
felt reflectively
strange now (really) speculative
in an isolation of aggression (secession)
and vibrant "youth cultures"
condensed into scents
that there never was
any resistance here
just a history of how
much I think
I hate it now
nervously waking
in older dead lives
piled into sodden republic
dumpsters as distribution deals
midway woods with moods
making a larger shard
harder than even
those little linked moments *(Überblick)*
that make up the past
dealt as the eighties
and all the lovely formative
checks (cheques) the tiny
scams the cabs the pubs

the discoveries of parts
of the port city that now are long
articulated into "the failure
of social housing" (rotting condos)
versus Karl Marx Hof
and the textual joke of "glocal"
would have then the styles
that seem determined and gooey
in comparison sombre
with the docks being a
working and not filming
area gone awash thinner
and able really
to "amble" in the class-
partitioned streets of the city
split east west
and the petty violences
as maybe now
intensities or so many flows
regarded with such
internal tension
and external torque
that easy hatred and lovely
disdain training in
typesetting or buildings as
vocation to can't
little utopic touches
of the total design work
making, history,
conditions, actions
under

Jacob Peter Neufeldt, 1890

- LEONARD NEUFELDT -

Weeks later he finds his way back
to the table under the willow,
his lungs bled clear and crusted
where they'd opened again like punctures,
and a hiss of thin pain emptied them.
My unremarkable great-grandfather,
greybeard Crimean craftsman in a family of faces
and dreary clothes, is still the first
to reach for knife and fork.
We know him by his open collar, black vest
buttoned too tight, and broad lapels turned
slightly up. Where he sits straight as an ordinance
is yesterday, all the moments passed on
like this — "a thousand years to God"
he would have said, in which things
are going to be abandoned, living things
that one's grateful for — eldest son and daughter,
land, political calm, tubercular wife,
the young calf asleep in the orchard shade,
twitching a fly from its ears.

It's up to us to make out other needs:
grape arbour leaning into itself
against the small table his wife used to cover
with oil cloth and set with plain white plates
and a small care at her mouth
when there were only two children;
garden fresh again, the weeds heaped
like vegetables on the path and growing limp
in the sun; two rows of black raspberries

no one is picking this year, saw-tooth thorns
and papery leaves of dying vines
hidden by taller, straighter shoots;
windbreak of propped apricot trees, their fruit
whispering hurriedly through leaves and then
the soft thud of imperfection you feel
when a fledgling falls from its nest;
thistle-free pasture sloping with certainty
to tamarind trees; blue dragonflies
depositing eggs on the water
where the river's green sleeves turn brown
from taking another twenty metres
of the pasture.

          The steep-gabled house sweeping up
behind the willow needs paint, and he'll hire
the Tatars he'd let go when they stopped
their roof repairs after one of them fell
like a chimney stone and the other two asked
to shore up instead the root cellar
collapsing on its south side,
the wall they'd rebuilt a year ago
with driftwood timbers. "Danger can be
a kind of faith, even if it doesn't better you,"
I imagine him shouting from the roof's metal-blazed
ridge at the end opposite the yellow softstone
chimney, to men not even family, men explaining
at first rudely with hands, in Russian,
and then in mysteriously simple harmonies
of Turkic vowels that it's time for dinner,
but they will return in a few days.

And so this evening is centred by where he is.
To his right his unsmiling wife stands
wiping her neck slowly like a humiliating wound.
To his left Grandfather, already eighteen,
is about to misname his ancestor four generations back
on the Vistula and slap the table over the mistake,

his error distilling what he needs to know
now that he has heard of cheap growing land
in valleys east of Samara and west of Orenburg.
In the margin Grandfather's sisters, younger than he,
lean away together, planning their lives
inside the torn edges, arranging the tiredness
the younger one always feels by the afternoon.

Jacob Neufeldt needs more than the simple glory
of what will be abandoned. He needs to rub
the future clear as his eyes, as an irony
just found out; he needs to be more careful
about letting on how much he wanted to come back
to this world, what directions his thoughts took,
how cool the air is in his lungs. He needs
to restore the shape of some things within,
their vengefully quiet outlines, sharper joys.
He needs to change the shape of things beyond
healing,
          to understand the moments
coming, the moments when we faltered.

Box Factory Girls

- LEONARD NEUFELDT -

Girls in bridal white blouses
walking to Guenther's box factory
when Bible School had closed
and azaleas opened like swans.
Bees hadn't yet roused berry fields
and no one else in town was hiring.
Not even guys with hopped-up cars
and open-throttle exaggerations
knew much about the box factory girls.

Inside the front door the girls exchanged
the fragrance of early morning muskrat grass
for the sweet astringency of freshly cut wood.
They stopped to watch two men,
nails in their teeth and brains, cobble raspberry flats,
side and bottom slats to grooved ends with shingle nails,
two hammer strokes per nail and taped fingers,
and then the crooning scream of the mill saw next door.

Below the loft to the right of the door
darkness stayed the whole day. Above the loft
light spilled through skylight windows
and wide cracks around them, and gathered flecks
of dust into lines that bent the loft's two-by-four
railing. Sandals clacking at the heels,
they mounted the ladder rungs
and held the second last one, looked up
as though to find a sunspot floating in the eye.

And then, at the top, their blouses caught
the light. They tied their hair up,
sat down straight backed,
napes stretched, arms forward,
before chest-high cast iron staplers,
heads ready to bob like pianists.
Three percussive notes: dismissively
they flung the box into the cage below,
a pint box of two pieces
stapled and tossed in a single motion.

The young man who started work before the girls
and lowered his eyes when they climbed the ladder,
sometimes every second rung,
increased the pace of his two-handed jamming,
six boxes at a time — hullocks we called them —
twice into each flat. He stacked flats
with fresh hullocks shiny as sap,
soon to be spotted with red stains
of the first picking.

As summer came on, another stapler was hired.
Fingers and pedal feet grew more desperate.
When the girls' eyes met,
heads would stop bobbing,
and they nodded sidelong to each other,
laughing soundlessly, keeping their secrets
in the loft till the dark rose from beneath
to disconnect their machines. They climbed
the ladder down, their feet slightly spread.

If the guys with cars stood in the doorway
or stepped inside to watch the girls descend
one after the other, the girls looked
at each other, retied their hair,
and knew exactly where to step in the dark
to leave through another door
and walk together on the cedar sidewalk

of Yarrow Central Road, past vague shapes
of church and Co-op Store and school,
toward the coming season.

Always they had their work cut out for them,
one day fastened to the next in quick succession,
tossed down to be assembled in larger frames
freshly numbered: love, double weddings
under twin arches, still births, many children,
parents sometimes senile, sometimes lucid
and wanting to die but saying so only to each other
and their daughters. Memories of hard work,
four foot stapler machines accompanying
the imagined, and the cage
full to the top with boxes by nightfall;
in the morning thinking of what will be,
walking a mile and more down Central Road
on the moss-bordered wooden walk,
picking white Yarrow flowers, flinging them aside
like raspberry boxes before they reached the door.

They'd look up the ladder where staplers waited,
where shiny slats were turned into boxes
and shadows into wind and hair into leaves
shivering against stems
when morning seeps like cold canal water
through berry rows and grows large as the field.
And their sandalled feet
counted the steps of the ladder again.

Opening a Boy's Book

- LEONARD NEUFELDT -

It begins as whistle-whir of grey,
becomes two mourning doves the boy
has startled out of a pear tree,
then the sky's sharp blue
leaving on wing tips. In the breathing
stillness, in the wind, a small shudder,
in the tree, the hum returning.
Turmoil of bumblebees rearranging blossoms
and the light in them — he counts to forty —
and some of the bees unhunch,
lift off drunkenly, drift down
to the lithodora's azure tremble of stars,
one flower, one bee, one breath.

—

Something like fear fevers his cheek
against his father's tweeded arm, the chest
behind the arm alive like a cello's strings
with the cadences of hymns,
above him a window's frosted bands of light,
beside him a morning rainbow
in the lacquered pew,
slow shimmer inside his breathing.

—

Pages of the book he used to take
to services are illustrated with flowers,
none alike. On the back flyleaf
a poem his father had written years before
he died. The boy had shown it to his friend,
who couldn't say why he had asked,
only a shrug as he leaned forward breathing
against the page:
There is a reason for absence in the heart,
For all that's missing and cannot return.
But if you think you are its meaning,
You will be alone in this world.

Standing in Line with Headset at the Monet Exhibit

- LEONARD NEUFELDT -

The pond wants to drop into the earth
and take the sky with it, utter sheen of light
that marks the distance to trees at the edge.

Between this morning's change and the far shore
the water is cold and deep. I'm standing here,
mired in mud, water seeping into my shoes,

feet and knees locked, ready for me to lean forward
with shears blunt as an unspoken prayer, wondering
which movement will reach and sever a veined stem

of the pond where a face floats upward among
the water's umbilicals, turns, fades the way it came,
as if weighted or afraid. But flowers of the pond

are dreaming slowly open — exiles returning
in ones and twos, coming furtively forward,
as in the story of a wide field, broken stone wall,

shoulder-high grass, twin towers of trees, a larger
monologue of blue, and children yearning toward it,
faces pale, smiling, others arriving on the margin.

The sun like a fire-bird, balancing picture and pond.
No wind to enter the quiet, no agitation from the deep.
The flowers are white. They've opened everywhere.

Why Our Town is Replacing Silver Maples with Better Trees

- LEONARD NEUFELDT -

Even people you trust say "times are tough"
and "money doesn't grow on trees."
Especially on silver maples and whatever steps out
of their long hollowness in ice storms,
or out of softer drumming as the wind
kicks up, turns jade-green before it steers
zigzag funnels past the wails
of sirens and unshingles everything.

You stand shoulder to shoulder
with trees pieced back together by surgeons,
like neighbours on the mend or stolen spouses,
but you're wary of them, of grief begging
for respect, of salvaging what was planted
by others before your time, of your sympathy
seeping through like sap in a tree's bark.

The Pentecostal mayor believed in the power
of words, total renewal, and getting things done,
and in his twelfth year (the term before
his indictment), promised lamp standards
in rows along with trees in a single-file
on all streets with wiring underground.
When the weather's right, lovers walk lamp
by lamp into the sun reddening toward
evening, past the long magenta newness
of the non-profit mental hospital
already closed, past the parking lot's

memory board of white lines,
vandalized gates and cyclone fence
to the weeds' flowering promiscuity
at the end of the road.

                Walk further, alone,
into the field where blue ash and hackberry
cluster close to a polygamous silver maple,
the late sun behind you, look quickly,
expecting nothing: there. Arteries quivering up
the sheen of trunk and lower stems,
a blue pulsing in one maple tree
like a shadow in wind gusts
before it gives way to a trepidation
of late flowers, fits of leaves, and large
seed wings totally divergent. The stem unbarked
by lightning surprises you, a bole split
to the roots, although on the side you came
the crown is round and full.

Below the tree in the vetch, blond grasses
and burrs, volunteers everywhere,
spines gleaming straight and to the point
like a grinning *praise the Lord* and some
pushing up a first fingernail umbrella of leaves;
antennae-long silver-green seedlings
testing the air outside the mouth-shaped
cavity eight feet up the trunk
like a zany sideway idea.

Who will save the silver maple from itself,
from streets paved with asphalt, concrete or gold,
or intricate words less wooden than trees,
rotting them at the heart, up and down?
You, standing half in the evening sun
and half in the shade wondering who deserves
this tree's manifest of messiness.

Stars West of Williams Lake

- LEONARD NEUFELDT -

"It is time for all the heroes to go home
if they have any, time for all of us common ones
to locate ourselves by the real things we live by."
— WILLIAM STAFFORD, "Allegiances"

The night a mountainside, the river somewhere
far below. I shouldn't expect more,
though prints toed down through the last
fragments of light and the pines' fragrance, down
to bleached rocks and stream and then the dark
seeping up the slope and a first star.

Thirteen billion years ago the stars were blue,
and many stars I see tonight from this cliff house
have no name, not even the reddest ones,
those letters and numbers memorized like words
of an old question, waiting for the crack of doom
inside a frozen silence, for star clouds
to stream out, skeins fine as gulls' spittle
woven and tied in place by invisible threads.

Follow them this way, along the Milky Way's
backbone, 100 billion globes
distending the night, down to the left: that's
Canis Major, and the dog Sirius,
the luminous one, nine light-years away,
far fewer in Huygens' measurements,
his explanations so precise and logical,
experts trusted him. After the great are forgotten
we relocate ourselves and whatever we've found.

Lower, at the end of the saw-edge black
of pine, aspen and spruce, far from Canis,
is Lupus: a stellar fire once burned
where the wolf star shines, heaven's holiest dog,
small but clearer than the hand of the god
it has severed. *Soon*, the prophet chanted. He meant
heaven and earth will be one except for the sea's
endless branches, and on that day the wolf
star shall be darkened by a salmon's murmurings,
the anguish of bears, and a fern root's secret,
but the prints I followed turned at the stream to lead
themselves back up a step ahead
of the dark, higher and higher, my breath racing
to catch up, to tell me the steeper a mountain
the more it refers to itself, and when
I stopped, the prints and night kept on going.

Sometimes the road to where you're going,
the straight-through one, is gravel, and it isn't
straight at all; in and out of sun and shade
it's hard to take in the country, and I chafed
at the wheel, dodging potholes and ruts drying
like day-old coffee. In the streams the road
followed, light flickered like stars suddenly
born and gone. And here, high above
the Chilcotin, my back against the door
of this low cabin still feels the curve of the driver's
seat and years of waiting to come here —
with no one else to explain what is or what
to expect, the cold spreading like breath past
fingertips, shivering toward trees
that touch the stars, and suddenly howls holding
long as though they have far to go, and answers
faint as an echo, slowly: two wolves
giving themselves away until nothing is left
but eyes stalking the sky like stars.

Bitez Beach: Namaz and Turkish Coffee at Dawn

- LEONARD NEUFELDT -

The muezzin's clamorous call to prayer
and young children startled awake
in the house behind me.
Today, perhaps, they will begin to know
themselves or the pilgrimage of breeze
caught up in white window lace
foreign as the language
I now sometimes dream in.

All-night bars and coffee houses
along the shore are closing, and stray dogs
stretch themselves on the boardwalk's
laddered dark, sniff the deeper darkness
of boards removed and paving stones
stacked like amphoras to replace them.
In the bay four yachts at anchor fretting quietly
in and out of time this side of dawn,
and a swimmer walking slowly, head down,
to the pier's far end, absorbing the immensity
of the muezzin's amen, the sudden hush,
the small dark rings where fish nosed up
to feed, and from the hills behind me
repetitions of a donkey's desire.

The outgone swimmer enters the dullness
in a watery half-halo, divides it
like a seal, changes course. Close to shore
a dragonfly's filigreed wings turn transparent
in a sudden slipstream of light.
The swimmer changes course a second time.

I find a key in my pocket and I know
where home is as I walk behind the stray dogs
and nod to the woman leaving the bakery,
a loaf in each hand, no need to shoulder anything.
I put away my notebook, no urge to take
loose patches of morning light and fill and fill
all that might be in between, to say that day
has arrived and needs an answer,
lest it mingle like Bitez with our bruised lives
neither simple nor just, or with the lifetimes
of children wakened by the muezzin,
impatient all at once and then with practice.

There are things that will not change today,
tourists coming and going, for example,
a town's name if it means heaven's door,
two Toronto journalists at the Shah Hotel
who agree each morning and each afternoon
on how different Canadians are from Turks,
construction workers sipping morning *chay*
through toothbrush-bristle moustaches
black as missing teeth or the small snake
that lives in the stone wall next door
and does no harm to anyone.
May it live for a thousand years.

Namaz: Turkish word for *Azan*, the Muslim call to prayer.

Non-Fiction

Limoncino Road

- PATRICK FRIESEN -

Sitting on my balcony sipping limoncino and listening to music. Limoncino is an Italian lemon-based liqueur that pours lemon sun into your guts as you drink it. Doing that, this afternoon, under a blue sky in Vancouver. Almost the blue I grew up with in Manitoba. And I've got Big Dave McLean singing the blues on the CD player; the sound of Winnipeg, that raw, intense, straight-forward integrity. Lucília do Carmo comes on, too, with "Maria Madalena." *Saudade*: not so much longing for a physical home, in this song, but the condition of longing that is inherent to passion and sorrow.

Sometimes you have to get to the point of enough. That lemon shine inside that can go anywhere, and sometimes you have to go way past enough. Sometimes you just have to get out of yourself, however you do it without harming yourself and, more important-ly, others. Sometimes, I suspect, you can't help but harm yourself before you get to where you're going. There's so much civilization, so much deception, to work your way through.

More than enough. That is the need of experience. Everyone's felt it; many have gone there for a while and returned, some didn't, others backed off, or put one foot in, testing the water. Going too far is dangerous, possibly physically but, more importantly, in other ways.

Beyond enough, and yet the poet needs to return from there and, knowing something about human beings and about craft, has to write a little less than enough. Just the right space or time between the two. Perhaps this is the crux of poetry. The poet has not only to leave, but create, room for the listener. There has to be a created space between the experience and the transmission of it. It can't be said like an equation. It's impossible, to begin with; language does not have that capacity. When someone tries to reproduce the experience, exactly, in language, you're left with bad writing.

The art is in writing less, in underwriting, but in underwriting with such skill that the listener will not only be able to fill the space but, more importantly, yearn to fill it. And, in filling that created space, the listener reaches his or her own experience beyond enough. This is the collaboration of poet and listener. How can anyone, unless they're easily sated by sentimentality, laugh or cry if everything is done for them? The held-back cry, that understanding, happens in that smallest of moments, of spaces, between the words and the experience.

Today I sip limoncino and live, briefly, in lemon fire. It can happen other ways, like writing out of late-night exhaustion. I get up and write some notes; phrases, thoughts, emerging that wouldn't have otherwise. The poem is rarely complete, and I know that. When I read the lines later, tomorrow, I may well see they are simply self-indulgent, excessive to a point beyond redemption. However, I may find it's all done or, more likely, there is something that holds within it the whole poem that has not yet been written. There's my work, to approximate the motion of my thinking of a few hours ago, or yesterday. Inevitably, it will find its own direction, possibly something quite different from what began.

By now I'm listening to another kind of music, *Spiegel im Spiegel*, by Arvo Pärt. Some of his writing agitates me in a way that does no good. But there are several sublime pieces, and this is one that speaks to that easy cliché of less is more, where some kind of excess is experienced, then reduced. The simplicity of the piano with the violin weaving in and out. I am given the gift of filling in the spaces where they need filling in, and leaving them where they need to be left. My heart is full, and my mind is quietly moving.

Great singers do the same thing. They chop the ending of a word, or they eliminate a word altogether. They pause within a line where other singers would not. The pause is held just long enough for you to want to fill it in, and perhaps you do. Perhaps you fill it just as the singer does and, at that moment, you and singer are one. You are singing the song, even if you are silent. Sometimes I think it's about the need, nothing else, the need for voice.

Voice, however, has various connotations. Voice can be the sound you hear, but it is also, if you find it, the fundamental self. The self that is always there amongst the many selves we develop. The one self that all the other selves refer to, emerge from. The one self that is you on earth, and possibly beyond.

And, I suspect, one has to find a way beyond enough to find this self. Paradoxically, going outside oneself, the self created by civilization, to encounter self. And I may just be talking about the fire; I may be talking about my visits via specific poems, phrases I hear in conversations, songs, certain voices, the trembling of aspen leaves, water in its variations. This hot afternoon I'm talking about Via Limoncino.

The Dog Outside the Dream

- PATRICK FRIESEN -

Broken out of the core of sleep by a dog's deep barking, he was instantly awake; he was aware of an image melting quickly away, an image of a dog, or wolf, standing in a field, gazing at him. He tried to hold on to this, wondering if it was a dream he had been drawn out of, or simply an image that arrived when he heard a dog barking down the street.

A dog in a field. Something primitive about it, at least for the few seconds the image remained. A dog, and a sense of danger. Was it danger from the dog, or a danger facing the dog? Death, he thought, something to do with death, or a death. Where was the dog standing? Had there been trees, or a building, perhaps, near-by? He thought a building, but already he felt he was adding details. Strange to be on the cusp like this, turning between where he'd just been and what he was already creating.

A man and a dog. A boy, actually. Or both. An immense aloneness, his aloneness, the dreamer's yearning. This he felt, and he knew it came from the dream. Even as the dream disappeared; in fact, all that was left now was the idea of a dog, not a dog itself, the loneliness from the dream. He didn't doubt that. And, he now understood that he would remember that he had dreamed a dog, though no picture remained in his memory.

He propped himself up on an elbow, snapped on the light, and tried to read the time on the alarm clock without putting on his glasses. The lamp's chain still moved, his eyes getting used to the sudden light. He thought he'd probably been awake for no more than two or three seconds. There was no barking through the window now, just the soft rustling of rain on leaves. Had the barking been inside the dream? Had a dog actually barked outside the window? For a moment he thought of one dog calling the other, but the thought drifted away.

Why did he yearn? Had he witnessed it? He had been in the dream, it was his dream, but had he been in it as a character, a participant? Even the longing was dissipating.

He wondered, now more widely awake, was it possible to not be having your own dream? Could you dream someone else's dream? Well, no. If you dreamed, it was yours, no? By definition. He tried to remember the thought from a moment before, it had been interesting, but he couldn't bring it back. It nagged him for a moment. He realized if he didn't go back to sleep immediately, he might not at all.

He switched off the light and lay back. Eyes closed, he tried to empty his mind. Was it his dream, or his residual memory of it, that occupied him, even as he resisted thinking? Was it the ideas cropping up now that drove him farther from sleep? His legs began itching. He knew this itch, and he didn't bother scratching. Once he began scratching, it was endless, and he'd draw blood. He remembered the thought he'd had; the notion that a dog not far from his window had barked in reaction to the dog barking in the dream. Perhaps this was reversed. Was one of the dogs a thousand years old, or older?

He sat up. There was not going to be sleep anytime soon. He felt a vague sadness, but he didn't know where it came from, nor whom he was directing it to, or should have been directing it to. Was it purely his own sadness? Well, one way or another, it was. It sat in him, his legs off the side of the bed, his hands holding up his head. He carried the sadness, wherever it came from. It was going to be his sad night. He stood, opened the curtains and looked up and down the street. Drizzle, almost a mist by now. Not a soul.

In the kitchen he poured water into a sauce pan, and turned up the element; then he reached for his favourite pale blue mug. He squeezed in some honey, then sat down on the couch in the living area. It was a one-bedroom apartment, not many steps from sleep to kitchen to the couch.

He wondered, sometimes, about his life in this space he lived in. He'd been alone for nine years. At first the apartment had simply been the relief of his own place. He loved solitude. It took some years before he began feeling like an older man. Old, in the sense of emerging quirks. He talked to himself fairly often. Not making decisions, or anything useful like that. Rather, stupid little conversations about things like putting down a book and getting up to prepare food.

"That's how it goes. Ah, the knee again. Tea? Yes, tea, but which one? How about a change, green tea; they say it's good for you . . . and honey this time, or sugar?" And he'd hum a song, a snatch of it.

And he was quite aware of his inconsequential talk, took some mild humour from it. Sometimes he wondered if it was advancing like a disease, and he'd become one of those men on the streets who walked alone having loud, often angry, conversations with an invisibility beside them.

Probably, he thought, this talking to self is inevitable when you live alone for a length of time. Not much social life; he went days without conversations. Greetings to Fortunato, the cheese man, certainly, but not much more. Human as suppressed social animal.

There was an aftertaste of loneliness. The water came to a boil as he became aware of his sharpened senses. He was noticing details, physical moments even as they passed. And he associated them with each other. The sound of the water from the boil, and that whispering sound of rain in the leaves. When he opened a pop bottle for a quick sugar dose, he noticed a momentary wisp of smoke rising. He liked to think it was smoke, but he knew it was some other scientific phenomenon. No, he knew it was smoke, and it was the smoke of yearning. It had been released. Intangible, except for that momentary swirl. This he knew. He carried it.

His work for this night, he thought, and he turned on the computer. He remembered his friend Ralph, who had told, in finest detail, the dreams he had each night. He had enjoyed Ralph telling some of them, but others brought a glazed look to his eyes. Only the details of one's own dreams retain one's total interest. Ralph wrote his down precisely, and he did it to this day. He believed Ralph could direct his dreams to some degree. An amazing dreamer.

He wasn't going to do that, had never done it, couldn't do it. He took what he could, even if it was a single image, or possibly a sound, and he built on that. It was the raw material for his work. He had no illusions that he was recording his dreams, or being true to them. What he did was flat-out betrayal. The dreams were fodder, not much more. Was this perhaps another kind of dreaming? What can you do with the fact of a dog, no longer seen, and an aftertaste of a miserable longing?

Whisper

- ANGELIKA DAWSON -

I live in a haunted body.

He comes some time in the night each May and I know that he's been there because I wake up with his name on my lips as if I've said it out loud.

Michael.

Over the years, his name has grown quieter there. At first, it was a screaming in my head, and I would wake with a start as if someone had yelled at me. For weeks his name would echo off the walls in my head like a shout in a canyon, Michael, Michael, Michael. Until it was gone.

Now his visit is a whisper.

Michael.

I can't tell if it's his voice or mine. I don't even know his voice. And when I hear his name, I'm not sure. Maybe it *is* Michael, speaking his own name, wanting to know that I won't forget him, that I won't forget he is still mine.

. . . I have called you by name; you are mine . . .

My first encounter with Michael was grim. The pain was everything; I could think of nothing else. I was drowning, unable to catch my breath, my legs and arms weak from pushing, my eyes burning from the sweat, blood-shot from straining. Even after he arrived, I couldn't yet consider Michael or hold him; I couldn't even look at him for the pain.

What went through Michael's mind that day? Was it strange to hear my familiar voice crying out after hearing it until then as quiet talking or the hum of a lullaby? Was it strange to feel his father's hands on his body? To hear his father's sobbing? Did he feel the bright light in the room, the cold air on his skin, a strange hunger for breath?

When the pain was finally gone, I held him, gasping. Michael was beautiful. His long fingers might have played the piano, cupped a basketball, caressed a lover. Fingers that should have, at first, instinctively curled around one of my own. His skin was so smooth, his body so perfectly formed, his tiny face so red and round.

It was hard to look at him, but I wanted his image burned into my mind. He was a gift and I wanted to remember. I thought that we wouldn't be together for long. I didn't know that he would be so persistent.

Michael caught us by surprise. He came early, so suddenly that we weren't ready for him. We didn't even know his name. But Aaron knew long before Michael arrived. "My brother Michael is coming," he would say. Months later, Aaron sat on my hospital bed, hugged Michael's still body and held his hand. But it wasn't enough for Aaron to see Michael's face. "I want to see you, Michael," he said. "Mom, I want to *see* him." Unwrapping Michael from his blanket, he touched his body and played with his toes. He talked and talked.

Michael was silent. He was already dead.

I wonder now how Aaron knew that our baby would be a boy,

that his name would be Michael. I wonder also why Michael visits only me. And why, when he visits, he is silent, except for his name.

. . . and I will proclaim my name . . . in your presence . . .

Michael means "image of God."

It's Michael! I'm home! It's not like an announcement: it's a whisper. *Michael.* I wake up in the echo of his presence. In those moments of half-sleep, the space between nothing and knowing, I am aware that I've heard something and that he's left again. Michael. I've tried keeping my eyes closed, to see if an image will rise, but it never does. I know that it never will.

. . . But you cannot see my face, for no one may see me and live.

There is no sadness in this. I've seen his face once and that is enough. And each May I am given all that I need. I live in the whisper of his name.

I Shall Not Want

- DEBORAH CAMPBELL -

My grandfather answers the doorbell. "God bless you, God bless you," he says, holding open the screen door and reaching out to embrace me. He is rickety, like scaffolding, and easily winded. My grandmother, standing behind him, is soft and plump. Her blue dress brings out the colour of her eyes.

I sit on the sofa beside my grandfather. His top teeth are paper-thin and the bottom ones are hollow, like empty wells. He says that first thing in the morning, when he wakes up, he recites the Psalms. The other day he was reciting Psalm twenty-three and he said, "The Lord is my shepherd, I shall not." He had forgotten the word that came next, so he recited it to himself in Gaelic and the word returned. It was right there waiting in the language of his childhood.

"Want. I shall not want."

Everything in their living room looks floral, a recent change. The gold shag carpet is now a soft plush pink. Relegated to the basement are the books I remember from my childhood, the complete set of Charles Dickens from 1923 that belonged to my great-grandmother and the Philharmonic organ with sheet music for "Auld Lang Syne." The bad landscapes painted by a relative, "the artist," still hang on the walls, but I miss the musty smell of old furniture mixed with Red Rose tea.

Their suburban bungalow is kept deliberately dim. My grandfather has only twelve percent of his vision remaining — by whatever standards one judges twelve percent: shadows, shapes, recognizing the colour red — but even so his eyes are light-sensitive, so we sit with our backs to the window. It is as if he is returning to the womb, preferring darkness to daylight. I take his hand and he presses mine. His touch is cool and dry.

He wants to know if I've found a good church and I tell him I have. I don't tell him it's the Church of Sleeping In On Sundays, because I don't want him to stay awake nights, worrying about the fate of my soul. As he grows older, he clings more tightly to religion. It is a bright candle in a dark and unknown place.

My grandmother rocks in her chair. We talk about my cousins: who has graduated, who has jobs, which one has boyfriends or girlfriends. The living room is busy with family photos. We gossip. We talk about my brother's leaky condominium, the result of shoddy construction, and my grandmother says that people these days don't seem to care about being honest. I ask her if she has people calling to try to get her credit card number, and she says yes, all the time, but she just hangs up.

Good, I say. You have to do that. I tell her about this show I saw that said seniors are particularly vulnerable to phone fraud because they were raised to be polite. My grandmother says it's worse when they come to the house, just trying to keep them outside the door. My grandfather, who has been leaning his head back as if asleep, murmurs, "But I've met so many nice people." His voice cracks at the edges. "I've been so lucky to know such nice people." He is always close to tears these days, no matter what the topic, even the morality of door-to-door salespeople. My grandmother says something about the way my grandfather thinks people are nice more often than it's true. He could see the good side of Charles Manson, and she knows it.

She pulls herself up to put on tea. I offer to do it, but she won't have any part of that. I take my grandfather's hand and we shuffle together, my arm supporting his back, to his chair at the dining room table. He is so thin that the bones of his thighs are sharp against the fabric of his pants. He wears orange plastic sunglasses to protect him from the light outside the window.

My grandmother puts out macaroons and blueberry scones on her best Royal Albert. She tells me that the pharmacist came to their home and went through my grandfather's prescriptions. He took thirty or forty vials of pills away in a plastic bag and left just three. There was concern my grandfather had been taking whatever he felt like on a given day, mixing and matching. But nothing seems to work anymore, in any case. There is no cure for the passage of time. My grandfather suffers a variety of vague, recurrent ailments — but more to the point, he is ninety-one. He is known for saying, "If I can just get over this hump. . ." Today he murmurs, almost to himself, "Maybe I won't get over this hump."

We hold hands to say grace. My grandfather blesses the food and thanks God for my presence. We pour milk into the teacups so it heats up gradually when the tea is added, and my grandfather pours, his frail hands trembling.

I ask what they are planning to do with the book collection in the basement. The books loom large in my childhood, the smell of yellowed paper like rich incense, the quiet afternoons spent turning pages under my grandparents' roof. I ask casually. I don't say, when you die, or after your death. My grandmother responds that the books belong to my uncle. I'm not sure if she understands what I am asking or which books I mean, but I can't rephrase or clarify my question. I wonder what I will have left of them when they're gone.

Sunflowers, St. Petersburg

- DEBORAH CAMPBELL -

The sunflower fields appeared unexpectedly along the road to St. Petersburg. Through the window of the bus, I watched them stretch their golden faces toward the thin October sun. They were radiant bursts of colour in otherwise desolate terrain. Later the bus stopped near a concrete building with tinted windows. I stepped out and was greeted by a single sunflower, blooming alone beside the building's entranceway, swaying higher than my head. I fished my camera from my knapsack and took a photograph.

St. Petersburg was the perfect city for me. It was vast and grey and had the anonymous bustle of any large urban centre, this one set against a backdrop of opulence. Yet it seemed strangely empty, the way certain buildings seem empty by virtue of every door being closed. I had taken the trip as a remedy for a bruised heart, and the city mirrored my sense of isolation. On the subway, passengers stared silently into the middle distance. On street corners, classical violinists played for spare rubles. When the group I was travelling with talked and laughed, our voices sounded tinny and loud. The air of sadness had an almost physical weight.

Our guide knew a Canadian woman living in St. Petersburg who volunteered at a local orphanage. Every week she went there to hold the children. If you don't pick them up, she explained to the group, they learn not to cry anymore. If we were interested we could join her, and early one grey morning a few of us, half-awake, straggled onto the bus.

The orphanage was a large, white institutional building that smelled of disinfectant. The head mistress, a sturdy matron who wore fuchsia lipstick and rouge with the enthusiasm fashionable among Russian women, ushered us upstairs to an activity room. Benches were set up in the back, and she indicated, through gesture and tone, that we should take a seat.

After a moment, a side door opened and a group of preschool-aged children filed in. A nurse unlocked a cabinet and each child selected a toy. The nurse put on music and the children began to dance, holding their toys out in front of them, hopping up and down. Their downy hair swooped and fell. After a few minutes, the nurse turned the music off and the children stopped dancing. She turned the music back on and they danced. Then off again and they stopped. When the performance was over, the children returned their toys to the cabinet and filed out.

The show was intended, I think, as a pageant to showcase their beauty and health. Perhaps it was offered to prospective parents or visiting officials. At the end we clapped.

The Canadian woman told us this was the best orphanage in St. Petersburg. The facilities were clean, the children sufficiently clothed and adequately fed, though often sick. Lots of chronic runny noses, the side effect of not enough physical touch. Not all the children were orphans, she added. Often they were another mouth their parents could not afford to feed. She hoped eventually to provide children with a toy of their own to keep, a stuffed animal to take to bed at night. As it was, even their little uniforms went into a communal laundry and were randomly redistributed.

We went downstairs to hold the children. I picked up a baby from a cot surrounded by metal bars. His dark eyes were solemn and impassive as I rocked him in my arms and stroked his cheek. He was maybe nine months old. He didn't make a sound.

A bell rang. A troupe of two-year-olds toddled over to a low table, pulled out miniature chairs, and sat down. They folded their hands and waited for the nurse to bring their soup. Bowls set down before them, the children spooned the soup carefully into their small oval mouths without spilling a drop.

In the afternoon we went outside where pre-schoolers in identical blue snowsuits played in an enclosed yard. I took a seat on a wooden bench, pulling my coat and scarf around me. A little girl, about three years old, approached the bench. She was playing with a label from a can. She turned it over and over and waved it in the air as she slowly circled me. When I opened my arms she climbed into my lap.

Once in my arms, she could ignore me. She faced forward, playing with the label. Every so often she leaned her head back to study my face. She chortled in Russian and presented me with the label, only to pull it back before I could touch it. This became a game. We played together for almost an hour: the label offered, the label pulled back, a ritual dance. Once she dropped the label and it wafted to the ground.

Sliding off my lap, she kept one hand on my knee and retrieved the label with the other.

A whistle blew. Tension shot up her back. The other children ran to slip their hands into the loops on a rope the nurse held out. But the girl did not move. The nurse called out, but the girl acted oblivious, engrossed in playing with the label. At last the nurse came over. The girl stiffened, then arched her back like a cat and screamed. The nurse took her from my arms and carried her wailing across the yard and into the building, her cries fading and then disappearing altogether.

It has been several years since my journey to St. Petersburg, but my memory of her remains. Her qualities were those the other children largely lacked: a refusal to be broken, the capacity to feel.

I marvelled at the strength of a three-year-old girl in a situation where most would have given up. How could I not face up to the minor adversities of my own life?

On my kitchen wall hangs the picture I took of the single sunflower on the road to St. Petersburg. It grew alone, like the girl in the blue snowsuit, and takes up the entire frame.

The Basket

- CONNIE BRAUN -

"A bruised reed he will not break . . ."
Isaiah 42:3

When I was very small I heard a story. "This will be the sky," said Miss Friesen, our Sunday School teacher. She ran her flattened hand over the light blue flannel cloth to smooth it, then pressed down strips of green felt and said, "And this is grass along the river bank." She positioned each cut-out from the Primary Curriculum Guide on the cloth-covered board. "Bulrushes. Basket. Miriam. And Aaron, see? He's hiding in the reeds, watching." We watched as another blue cloth turned into the Nile River. Miss Friesen was explaining the story of Moses, who grew up to bring his people out of the land of suffering.

This story of a baby hiding from Egyptians in a floating basket captivated me. We had a basket at home! One large enough to hold a baby. In the backyard on laundry day, I drifted away in the basket beneath trousers, shirts and underwear that waved shamelessly in the breeze.

At such times my young mother wore a home-sewn cotton dress to do her housework — not the shapeless cleaning dress worn by older Mennonite women, but a sleeveless Canadian *Hauskleid*, hemmed above her bare knees. Mother sprayed Adorn on her back-combed hair, letting it fall to her shoulders instead of pulling it back into a bun. And she wore a hair-band, not a kerchief to cover her head, just like the actress on "That Girl" on T.V. An attractive, modern wife despite her plain sounding name, Erna. Prettier than the friendly neighbour lady with a boy's name, Bert, who smoked, had a husband named Scotty and belonged to a bowling team but no church.

We lived in a subdivision made up of box houses all built by my father, with English-speaking neighbours on either side, clotheslines spanning backyards and Scotty's Stanfield's and Bert's Wonderbras dancing on the lines on laundry day.

Under our own clothesline sails, I sat in the stern of our wicker basket, my spindly legs extended to the bow as I clutched the braided edge. The basket flexed and creaked as I rocked side to side and imagined the grass was a swift river or wild ocean.

"Time to come out," Mother said all too soon. She took the sunshine-smelling clothes from the line and placed them in the basket to carry indoors. As her ironing filled our kitchen with laundry scent, I played underfoot. We spent our mornings together while Father built houses.

Now this basket is mine, though Mother gave it to her sister after we children were all grown, and my parents moved from the family home Father had built to a smaller upscale apartment, again built by our father. My mother held a garage sale and marvelled over "the things people buy!" But her sister Ella must have noticed the basket. I can imagine the conversation:

"What are you doing? You shouldn't sell this, Erna. It's still good!"

"Well, what would I want it for? It takes up so much room!"

"If you're going to get rid of it, I'll take it."

"Well then, take it."

Next, the sisters would have stifled their giggles until they shook, then laughed aloud, slapping their thighs. Laughing at themselves and their Mennonite ways, wiping their eyes with the back of their hands. The things people buy. Getting rid of good things.

My parents came from another time and place. My mother was born in Poland in 1939, six months before Hitler's invasion. Her family's ancestors had lived in the same village near Warsaw, the German part of Wymisle, for generations. Unlike my father, Mother doesn't talk much about her early life. "Who wants to remember the bad things anyway?" When the war was in its final hours, her family tried to walk out of Poland across the frozen Vistula River. Erna was almost six, with thick braids and skinny arms and legs.

"The border was closed, *they* took everything and sent us back," she remembers. When the family returned to the village, their house was empty. Plundered. Soon after, family members were seized, her father taken to prison camp, all the children except the youngest distributed to work on Polish farms.

"I gathered wood for the stove, brought in water, looked after children smaller than me. I herded geese. And everyone helped harvest potatoes. In spring and summer I herded cows, monstrous cows. I was afraid!"

Father was born in the Ukraine where the slow-moving Dnieper flowed, after the "golden era," after the Revolution and the "exodus." He was born during the 1931 famine, brought on by forced collectivization, in fertile grassy steppes where wheat and other grains and orchards flourished. Stalin was in power.

Both my parents fled their homeland as refugees. One boy and one girl among millions caught in the crossfire of Hitler and Stalin. They layered on their summer and winter clothes and carried meagre parcels of food. As armies approached and bombs fell, dislocated villagers could take only what they could carry by hand or push in a peasant's handcart. Anything of use was soon worn out, lost or stolen along the pockmarked trail from Eastern Europe to the West.

The wicker basket is surely one of the few surviving items that holds the past. A refugee boy wove it from tender white willow now dark with age, crafting it into a large oval with twisted handles at each end.

After I grew up and moved from home, the basket faded from my memory. But one day, as my two young sons and I were visiting Aunt Ella, she brought it out to use as a makeshift playpen, then poured us a cup of coffee. I was amazed to see it again. My little boys, one blonde, one dark haired, clambered in, sat facing one another, plump hands clutching the sides while rocking wildly side to side in opposite rhythm.

"Bigger! More!"

"See me, Mommy!"

Once more the basket became a vessel in which delighted toddlers giggled like happy sailors.

"Father made this basket," I said. "I wonder why Mother would give it away."

"I know," she replied, "look how well it's made. I was surprised your mother didn't want it anymore, but . . . here, why don't you have it now?"

I assumed that my father made the basket before he and his mother and three sisters boarded the transport ship *Samaria* in Cuxhaven, forty miles north of Bremerhaven, on the North Sea. From there they sailed through the Channel, then across the Atlantic and into the Gulf of St. Lawrence, to unknown Canada — in a transport loaded with survivors and ghosts, hope and finality. My father's father died of cancer before the departure, was left behind in a Catholic cemetery in Salzburg with payment to maintain the plot for the next ten years, a timespan which, to his youngest son, seventeen at the time, must have seemed like forever. Father's brother lay beneath a field somewhere in Poland. Without a grave marker to visit someday, that parting must have been an even sharper farewell. Another brother, first forcibly conscripted, then a prisoner-of-war, remained behind for awhile, since Canada would not yet accept former enemy soldiers. My father, Peter, was now the man of the family.

Peter learned to weave baskets in 1946, when his shattered family was resettled in eastern Austria in a zone that had been occupied by Soviet forces. In a fortunate transfer of territory, it was taken over by the British, though later many refugees were nevertheless repatriated to the USSR under the Allied agreement.

"I was fifteen," he tells me, "I wanted to go to school but I couldn't."

"Why not?" I ask him, as though it were a simple matter. "Too old?"

"I wasn't too old, I was forbidden. I was considered a German refugee."

His education had been disrupted, first in Russia by the Bolsheviks in Rosengart, the Mennonite village quaintly named after a rose garden, then altogether by war. Instead of a student, he was a farmhand working for rations, doing a grown man's portion of work without receiving a man's wage: swinging a scythe, cutting wide swatches of meadow and gathering them with a rake fashioned from wood, creating section after section of hay mounds resting on hillsides like sleeping giants. Twenty-seven cents an hour for eight hours of labour seems too meagre to get by on.

An older refugee, also from southern Russia, was a basket-maker by trade. Mr. Goertz struck an agreement with Peter to sell baskets for him: functional containers for firewood, potatoes, orchard apples or wash-worn clothing. So on Saturday and Sunday Peter would take baskets to the alpine farms around the city of Murau, to the stout farm wives, *Bäuerinnen*, sturdy enough to plough fields, milk cows and butcher pigs, but who seldom ventured to the village ten kilometres down the path. Peter sold baskets or traded them for meadow-sweetened butter and marbled slabs of pork, earning enough to supplement his family's paltry food rations.

At the start, Peter sold Mr. Goertz's baskets, then realized he could earn more if he made his own. On his days off, he spent hours on the banks of a nearby river cutting strands from weeping willows, his fingers green as fresh spring manure. For finer baskets, he boiled the branches to loosen the bark, then peeled it off to expose the smooth white tendons of wood beneath. He was quick to learn. He fashioned a framework from cords of willow strung together. Around the perimeter, through this framework, in and out, he threaded the willow. Around and around. At a height of three inches he tapped down the branches with a mallet, repeating the procedure until the height and depth were right. Finally, he selected another two strong strips, cutting them into the appropriate lengths and looping them through the rim of the basket at one end. Joining these, he wound them together, smooth as rope, threading them back into the rim for a handle.

"Ah, jetzt kommt der Korbmacher!" the farmwives exclaimed as they welcomed him. Did they feel sorry for the boy with eyes like morning mist, who trudged all the way to their mountainside farmhouses with a stack of baskets and his tales of the war and a faraway place? Well-told stories that caused them to pause from their chores. An escapee from Russia . . . caught on the front . . . Russians on one side . . . Germans on the other!

"You walked from Yugoslavia?"

"Yes. Through the pass; they forced us. My mother was ill . . ."

". . . and with a small child yet! How did you manage?"

"I begged for food along the way . . . just some milk or bread."

When Peter told stories, even the men paused from their work, leaning against the fence posts to listen.

I wonder if he told them the unimaginable, harrowing parts, the silent gaps like pages torn from the book of his life: "A firing squad . . . *Pa* pulled me close, whispered to me, 'Run when they start to shoot. Find your brothers! And when they look for us after the war, tell them what happened to our family.' But I couldn't think of being the only one left. At the last moment they didn't shoot us."

They. The villains of such stories are always nameless.

The farmers then sealed their transactions with a slice of black bread topped with smoked bacon and a swallow of home-made Schnapps that took Peter's breath away.

A Hungarian refugee working on the same estate taught Peter another skill, growing tobacco. Together they cut the plants, sorted the leaves, sprinkled them with sugar-water, then dried them. Peter learned how to roll cigarettes, emptying the boxes of perfectly rolled *Englischer Feingeschnitt* from the British care packages and placing his cruder home-made brand inside. Since he didn't smoke, he sold the finer cigarettes separately, piece by piece, for a premium.

There he stood at the farmer's market, the lanky boy with his stack of baskets, packages of cigarettes hidden between them. It was from selling baskets and black market trading that he earned the money for the family to travel repeatedly to the immigration office in Graz to get their emigration papers in order.

But my basket wasn't crafted in Austria. Recently my father corrected my version of history. He had woven it in the New World, in the valley carved from the river that gave it its name. After coming to Canada, Father first settled in the Fraser Valley, among Mennonites in a farming community. He made the basket in 1948 out of willow branches taken from the pooling waters along the banks of the smaller Vedder River. "Why should I care about that basket?" Father would wonder. To him it was only one of many baskets he'd made when he was young.

"And what a pain it was to make!" he chuckled. "The branches were too tough to pick. My fingernails were always dirty, and peeling the bark took forever. In Canada I found all kinds of jobs other than weaving baskets, for better money."

I envision my father back then. An intelligent, unschooled seventeen-year-old survivor with the long slim fingers of an artist . . .

Along with his basket-making skill, he brought with him across the ocean the know-how to start again. I imagine him meeting Erna, the shy Mennonite girl whose life had also been displaced. DPs, people called them. Young immigrants speaking the wrong language — though they would someday wish that their children were fluent in it and that their grandchildren could understand it. Father did not continue weaving baskets, but he built houses using the same principles. For his Canadian children, his hard work provided playthings, education and vacations. A good start.

I must admit the basket, still durable after all these years, is not prominently displayed in my home; in fact, I don't even use it for laundry. In it I store all manner of things that we casually accumulate, things that we use only seasonally: hockey skates and ski hats;

roller blades, baseball gloves and a soccer ball. But I remember playing in that basket, Mother standing at the clothesline. By that time I spoke English to her and she to me. After all, we were Canadian.

Moving Homes

- BARBARA NICKEL -

We glimpse the blunt spires of an iceberg hiding behind South Twillingate Island. Plans for the evening are abandoned; we take car and camera, drive through the towns of Twillingate and Durrell, park near French Beach and hike up the rocky hill on a footpath hemmed by harebells, juniper, and partridge-berry low to the ground and not yet ripe. At the top, our prize: a white palace two kilometres offshore. We watch a speedboat the size of a beetle progress toward it, stop within a safe distance and slowly circle the domain.

How long since it calved from Greenland's thousands-year-old-glacier? It takes an iceberg two or three years just to reach the mouth of the fjord and enter Baffin Bay. It then begins a long journey, floating with a current that first takes it north, then eventually south to this coast and, if it lives long enough, to the Gulf Stream, where it will finally melt. What roofs and blue-tinged rooms, crevices, pillars and peaks has the ice built and lost along the way?

I've lived here in Twillingate, Newfoundland, for less than a week. When we have enough photos of this iceberg, the jagged islands, the sunset-drenched sky, we head down the hill for home: a basement suite the hospital has given to us for the summer and early fall, when I'll travel back to St. John's. At the annual Twillingate Hospital Fish and Brewis Dinner, I hold my plastic fork over a mass of white fishy mush topped with scruncheons (bits of pork fat) and think about how to answer the question asked by the nurse sitting next to me: "Where are you from?"

I might answer St. John's, where I have a permanent address, but she won't believe me — my accent lacks that tumble over hills and hollows; my fork is far too hesitant above this fish and brewis. I fall firmly into the category Newfoundlanders call "C.F.A.," which stands for "Come From Away." If I live out the rest of my days on this rocky island, listen at night to the wind bleating down power lines and heaving up the sea, if I track the years through ripened partridgeberry and freezing rain, through lilac and fog and picking mussels from rocks in cold July water to my knees, I will still be a C.F.A. And my children, and their children? How many generations does it take to be "from here?"

My maternal grandfather, John D. Janzen (1904–1976), felt that he was a C.F.A. to the *Tiefengrunders* he lived and worshipped with for fifty years. Born and raised in the Mennonite community of Bohnsackerweide, formerly part of the Danzig Free State and now part of Poland, he grew up swimming in the Baltic Sea (with a rope dividing the Men's Side from the Ladies' Side), finding stones of precious amber on the beach, learning how to dance a Strauss waltz properly in a tux and gloves, working his father's land, knowing that because of an older sister it would never be his.

He was twenty-one when David Toews visited from Canada and told of the cheap farmland in Saskatchewan. As my grandfather gazed out the window on the night before his departure in 1925, how did he picture the prairie? A place without that slope of blossoming pear and plum, apple and cherry, without the sea crashing just beyond that strip of fertile land, a place without his family.

He raised his own family in Tiefengrund, which means "deep ground," a community of farms near Laird, Saskatchewan. A tight clan, all those Friesens and Regiers, an island of people in the midst of fierce winters and unreliable crops. He married Elma Regier in the Tiefengrund Rosenort Mennonite Church, and every Sunday they drove with his horse and buggy and later a car up that gravel lane to worship there by the pines.

Under them he's buried. I've listened to their creak in the wind, smelled the wild roses he loved, wondered how he could live most of his life in a place and never feel at home. Was his position as an outsider to the *Tiefengrunders* around him simply his own perception? Or was my grandfather's homesickness so strong that for fifty years it created a barrier between himself and the community, as well as a "home" of memory within him? The ache of missing sisters, the memory of a waltz, the taste of sea carried along through all the chores and church basement suppers of his prairie life.

He'd thought of moving to British Columbia, with its flowers and ocean. My last address, before the one in St. John's, was in Vancouver, where I lived for nine years. It's a city of C.F.A.s; I met few people actually born and raised there. I should have felt at home. From my attic room on Adanac Street I had a view of the North Shore mountains, Burnaby and Stanley Park. Summers I'd lean out the open window and watch the annual fireworks scratch colour over the downtown sky. I hiked up the mountains, cycled the streets, wrote my first book, got stuck in traffic jams, endured months of rain and got married in Vancouver. It was never home.

"Where are you from?" asks the nurse. An alarmingly large mound of the white stuff still untouched on my plate.

A small place, only about 1,600 people. Billboards along the highway leading to town. One grain elevator left. Railroad tracks, crocuses in the ditch in spring. Main Street, Railway Avenue. A swimming pool, screams and laughter all summer long. Across from the park is a house made from old bricks once manufactured in the town. My initials and those of my siblings are scratched into the back sidewalk by the porch. Upstairs, in what was once my room, is an old red rug with little raised islands on it and out the window, through tangled vines, is a view of two tall pines and the curling rink. At night there are creaks in the radiators, sometimes the faint squeak of bats in the walls. This is where I am from. Or was.

Once, after my parents had sold the place and moved to Saskatoon, we visited the town on Christmas Eve and I walked to the house. It was the kind of December evening on the prairies that feels like brittle glass — the hoarfrost on the trees, the icy road, even the stars felt as if they could be shattered by a touch. I stood at the end of the driveway and watched my house. No one was home, but a dog barked from inside the garage. I looked up at my dark window, noticed the removal of vines. The dog barked again. I remembered — or was it simply the memory of a story once told to me — carrying a broken wine bottle up the driveway to the garbage bin at the age of three and accidentally cutting my wrist. I still have the scar. The dog barked again, more fiercely this time: *Go away! Don't you realize this is no longer yours?* I ran away.

Today we climb the hill again and see that the iceberg has disappeared. Perhaps it melted in these waters. I'd like to think that it's only travelled on a little farther with the current, out of sight to us, a whole house of ancient ice still on the move. It carries with it the scrape of rocks and a memory of falling snow, communities it passed years ago in Greenland and Labrador, the feel of sea bottom, the sound of gulls. It keeps on moving and changing, releasing its stories to the sea.

ABOUT THE CONTRIBUTORS

LEANNE BOSCHMAN's poems have been published in *Room of One's Own*, *Prism international*, and *Rhubarb*. Of her writing she says, "I write about the texture of life in a small coastal town. The voices and rhythms of the rain pervade my poems and become a motif for cycles of growth, decay, seasons of nature and stages of life, beauty and desolation." Born and raised in Saskatchewan, Leanne lives in Prince Rupert, where she teaches English at Northwest Community College.

CONNIE BRAUN, an emerging writer in Abbotsford, re-discovered her passion for creative writing at mid-life. While enrolled in the Humber School of Writing, under the mentorship of John Bentley Mays, she completed her father's memoirs. An avid traveller, she toured Russia last summer with her family and parents. This tour included a visit to the site of her father's lost home. Connie is on the board of directors of MORE THAN A ROOF, a non-profit housing society.

DEBORAH CAMPBELL is an intrepid journalist and author of *This Heated Place* (Douglas & McIntyre, 2002), a literary exploration of Israel and

Palestine. Her writing has appeared in the *Guardian, Adbusters, Utne, Modern Painters* and the *Walrus,* and her radio documentaries have been broadcast on National Public Radio and CBC Radio. She teaches literary non-fiction at the University of British Columbia and has guest lectured at Ryerson, University of Waterloo and Harvard. She recently returned from a six-month journey through Iran.

ANGELIKA DAWSON is a freelance writer and editor, columnist for *Timbrel* and former regional editor for the *Canadian Mennonite.* She has studied both fiction and non-fiction writing at Simon Fraser University, most recently working with Vancouver writer Nancy Lee. She is currently writing her first novel. Born in Winnipeg, Angelika grew up in Vancouver ("it still feels like home") and now lives in Abbotsford, BC.

JEFF DERKSEN, an Assistant Professor in Simon Fraser University's English Department, received the Dorothy Livesay BC Poetry Prize in 1991 for his first book *Down Time* (Talonbooks, 1990). He is a founding member of Vancouver's writer-run centre, the Kootenay School of Writing, and he has worked as an editor for *Writing Magazine.* His latest book is *Transnational Muscle Cars* (Talonbooks, 2003). He is also a contributor to *Stan Douglas: Every Building on 100 West Hastings* (Arsenal Pulp Press/Contemporary Art Gallery, 2003).

PATRICK FRIESEN lived most of his life in Winnipeg, Manitoba. He has taught creative writing at Kwantlen University College in Vancouver for the past ten years. His most recent works are *the breath you take from the lord* (Harbour Publishing, 2002), *calling the dog home* (CD collaboration with Marilyn Lerner, piano; Peggy Lee, cello; Niko Friesen, drums) and *Interim: Essays & Mediations* (Hagios Press, 2006). His book *A Broken Bowl* (Brick Books, 1997) was short-listed for the Governor General's Literary Award.

CARLA FUNK was born and raised in Vanderhoof, BC, and now lives in Victoria, where she teaches writing at the University of Victoria. In addition to appearing in various literary magazines and anthologies, she has published two poetry collections: *Blessing the Bones into Light* (Coteau Books, 1999) and *Head Full of Sun* (Nightwood Editions, 2002). A new volume of poems, *The Sewing Room,* is scheduled for release by Turnstone Press in the fall of 2006.

MELODY GOETZ is a Saskatchewan-born writer and painter now living in the Fraser Valley. She works with seniors in retirement community settings — and loves it! Her work has appeared in *Grail, Grain, Prairie Fire, Antigonish Review, Border Crossings,* in numerous anthologies, and in her chapbook, *train to Mombasa* (PunchPenny Press, 2000).

DARCIE FRIESEN HOSSACK was born and raised in Swift Current, Saskatchewan, a place that continues to inspire her writing. Darcie has won two short-fiction writing competitions and was nominated for the Journey Prize Anthology in 2004. A student in the Humber School of Writing and mentored there by Sandra Birdsell, she is completing a manuscript of short stories. Darcie is also a food columnist and travel writer for several newspapers in Kamloops and in her hometown Kelowna.

MARYANN TJART JANTZEN grew up in the small rural Mennonite community of Greendale, BC, with a book in one hand and a flower in the other. Currently, in addition to spending as much time as possible gardening and grandparenting, she teaches English and co-directs the Writing Centre at Trinity Western University in Langley, BC. She is also co-editor of a forthcoming volume of biographies of early Mennonite settlers in Yarrow, BC.

OSCAR MARTENS is the author of *The Girl with the Full Figure Is Your Daughter* (Turnstone Press, 2002). Oscar's fiction appeared recently in the *Malahat Review* and *Descant.* In 2006 he was nominated for the Journey Prize Anthology and the National Magazine Awards. Currently living in Burnaby, Oscar was born in Winnipeg and has resided in Victoria, Ottawa, Kenya and New Zealand, working as a deckhand, secretary, telephone solicitor, door-to-door sales person and farm hand.

ROBERT MARTENS was raised in the Mennonite village of Yarrow, BC, then known as "the centre of the universe." He fast-forwarded several centuries when he attended Simon Fraser University during its most tempestuous years. Recently he has helped write and edit several local histories in an attempt to slow our relentless blacktopping of the past. He also continues to wage the battle of the losers by writing poetry in his spare time. He lives in Abbotsford, where he works for Canada Post.

ELSIE K. NEUFELD grew up on a farm that straddled the line between Clearbrook (then Mennonite) and Abbotsford (all others). Her mother told sad stories about *Russland, Kommunismus, Hungersnot* and *Die Flucht,* while Father wept over war movies and letters postmarked Siberia. Sunday nights and writing letters to relatives overseas have merged in memories that continue to fuel Elsie's passion for life-stories. A published poet, personal historian, writing teacher and editor, Elsie lives on Sumas Mountain.

LEONARD NEUFELDT, a retired literary and cultural historian in New England studies, was born and raised in Yarrow, BC, and now lives just south of the border. His *House of Emerson* (University of Nebraska Press, 1982) received the *Choice* "Best Academic Book" national award in 1983, and his *Raspberrying* (Black Moss Press, 1991) was a nominee for the Gerald Lampert Award. Some two hundred of his poems have appeared in serials throughout Canada and the USA. His work has also been published in Europe, the Far East and India.

BARBARA NICKEL won the 1998 Pat Lowther Award for her first collection of poetry, *The Gladys Elegies*. Her work has also won the *Malahat Review*'s long poem prize and has appeared in many magazines and anthologies. A new poetry collection, *Domain*, is forthcoming in 2007. Her latest novel, *Hannah Waters and the Daughter of Johann Sebastian Bach* (Penguin, 2005), was a finalist for the Governor General's Literary Award and received the Sheila A. Egoff Children's Literature Prize in 2006. Born and raised in Saskatchewan, Barbara now lives in Yarrow, BC.

LARRY NIGHTINGALE was raised in Yarrow, BC, and is now a Vancouver resident. He works in the library/research field. Acknowledging a debt to the vital hum of his 1950s-era Mennonite community's hymns and prayers, the rattle of the '60s late night rock 'n' roll radio poets, and the metaphysics of Blake, Muir, Eliot et al., he pays attention to the rhythm and power of language. He has published in *W 49*, *Rhubarb* and *The Dry Wells of India* (Harbour Publishing, 1989).

LYNDA GRACE PHILIPPSEN was born and raised on Vancouver Island and now lives near Vancouver. Lynda writes poetry, fiction and essays, as well as reviews which have appeared in *Kyoto Journal: Perspectives from Asia*, *Books in Canada*, the *Vancouver Sun*, and *Arc Poetry Online*.

LOUISE BERGEN PRICE was born in an Austrian refugee camp and grew up in Abbotsford, where she still resides. Her writing explores her family story before and after the Mennonite diaspora from Ukraine. She has recently completed *All the Best People are in Prison*, a novel based on her mother's experience as a young girl. Louise serves on the board of the Mennonite Historical Society of BC and edits its newsletter, *Roots and Branches*.

AL REMPEL grew up as a Mennonite in Arnold, BC, and now lives in Prince George. He enjoys kicking about in the litter of the forest, looking for stories and metaphors he can use in his poems. Al is the author of the poetry chapbooks *Sumas Flats* (2004) and *Black as Crow* (2006). His poems have appeared in *Grain*, *Down in the Valley* (Ekstasis Editions, 2004) and *Forestry Diversification Project* (University of Northern British Columbia, 2006).

ANDREAS SCHROEDER has been writing full-time since 1971: fiction, non-fiction, poetry, radio drama, journalism, translation and criticism. He has written more than twenty books. Annick Press has published his two Young Adult non-fiction books: *Scams!* (2004) and *Thieves!* (2005). A novella, *Renovating Heaven*, is forthcoming. Andreas lives on the Sunshine Coast and holds the Maclean-Hunter Chair in Creative Non-Fiction at the University of British Columbia. *Shaking it Rough* (Doubleday, 1976) was shortlisted for the Governor General's Literary Award.

MELANIE SIEBERT, who is originally from Saskatchewan, now lives in Victoria, where the rivers run all winter. She graduated from the University of Victoria's Creative Writing program and is now probably holed up with her laptop, unless she's floating down an arctic river somewhere north and windy. Melanie's poems have been published in *Martlet*, *Geist*, the *Malahat Review*, *This Side of West* and *Echolocation*.

ROXANNE WILLEMS SNOPEK has published more than one hundred and fifty articles in North American and Australian periodicals as well as five non-fiction books for *Amazing Stories* (Altitude Publishing). Her mystery novel *Targets of Affection* (Cormorant Books, 2006) is the first in a series set in the veterinarian world. The idea for her short story "Two Steps Forward" came in a crowded hospital room, after the birth of her third daughter. Born and raised in Saskatchewan, Roxanne lives in Abbotsford.

HARRY TOURNEMILLE, who is inspired by the constant tension between the rational mind and the divine, shifted from theology to creative writing after a brief pastoral internship at the Mennonite church in his hometown of Grand Forks (his father was Doukhobor). Married, he now lives in Surrey, studies writing and philosophy at Kwantlen University College and is a landscaper in Vancouver. This is his second publication.

K. LOUISE VINCENT (formerly Schmidt), a Gabriola Island resident, was born in Pine Falls, Manitoba, where dreaming was linked to forests and fields. Her poetry has appeared in various literary journals and anthologies. Her books are *Hannah and the Holy Fire* (Oolichan Books, 2004), *Transforming Abuse: Nonviolent Resistance and Recovery* (New Society, 1995), and *The Green Room* (Leaf Press, 2005). She has just completed a new collection of poems, *The Discipline of Undressing.*

JOE WIEBE was born in Ontario and has lived on the West Coast since 1991 except during an eighteen-month "lapse of reason" in Winnipeg. He lives in Vancouver, where he recently completed his MFA in Creative Writing at the University of British Columbia. His novel *Mudville* was shortlisted in the Three-Day Novel contest in 2005. Joe has published more than one hundred articles in Canadian periodicals, including the *Vancouver Sun,* the *Globe and Mail, Geist, enRoute* and *Toro.*

RON J. WIEBE's remarkable short fiction was brought to our attention by Andreas Schroeder after the two met in a writing workshop. Ron's Saskatchewan roots and religious upbringing figure prominently in his stories. His short stories and satire have been published in *Image: A Journal of Arts & Religion, The Anthology of the Surrey Writers' Festival* and *The Door.* He also writes on wine, food and business ethics, in that order.

PUBLISHING CREDITS

Ronsdale Press would like to thank all the editors and publishers who generously allowed us to include their authors' works in *Half in the Sun*. A complete list of publishing credits follows.

LEANNE BOSCHMAN
"night rain" previously published in *PRISM international*. "this traffic," "West Coast Winter Solstice" and "night rain" are part of "Rain Journal Poems." "You are Here" is from "Landscape Redefined," a mixed media series with painter Edward Epp (acrylics and charcoal on canvas).

CONNIE BRAUN
"The Basket" previously published in *Rhubarb*.

JEFF DERKSEN
"In the Age of Megastructures"; "Someone like You"; "Sly Consumption Side Sentence"; "Everybody's Happy Nowadays"; "Space Replaced (over Time)" previously published in *Transnational Muscle Cars* (Talonbooks, 2003).

DEBORAH CAMPBELL

"Sunflowers, St. Petersburg" previously read on CBC Radio; "I Shall Not Want" previously published in *Geist.*

PATRICK FRIESEN

"Limoncino Road" and "The Dog Outside the Dream" previously published in *Interim: Essays & Mediations* (Hagios Press, 2006).

CARLA FUNK

"Faspa" and "Bums" previously published in *Blessing the Bones into Light* (Coteau Books, 1999); "Revelations, Age Eight" and "Doxology" previously published in *Head Full of Sun* (Nightwood Editions, 2002).

MELODY GOETZ

"by any other name" previously published in *Grain*; "watermark & new world" previously published in *Prairie Fire*; "Deen's Diner" previously published in *Border Crossings.*

OSCAR MARTENS

"Safe Places on Earth" previously published in *The Girl with the Full Figure is Your Daughter* (Turnstone Press, 2002).

ROBERT MARTENS

"mittagschlaf" previously published in *Rhubarb.*

ELSIE K. NEUFELD

"Moment 3" previously published in *Down In The Valley* (Ekstasis Editions, 2004); "Yesterday's Kill" previously published in Surrey Writers' Festival Anthology (2001); "What's Memory" previously published in *Breaking the Surface* (Sono Nis Press, 2000).

LEONARD NEUFELDT

"Box Factory Girls" previously published in *Raspberrying* (Black Moss Press, 1991); "Jacob Peter Neufeldt, 1890" previously published in *Car Failure North of Nîmes* (Black Moss Press, 1994).

BARBARA NICKEL

"Borscht" excerpted from "Komm, Essen," previously published in *The Gladys Elegies* (Coteau Books, 1997); "Homes" previously published in *Rhubarb* and *Books in Canada*; "Manifesto" previously published in *Rhubarb*; "Sestina for the Sweater" previously published in the *Malahat Review*; "Moving Homes" previously published in *Rhubarb.*

LARRY NIGHTINGALE
"Cathedralesque" from "Song from the Lofts (A Poem Cycle)," excerpt previously published in *Rhubarb*; "Riding Freehand" previously published in *W 49*.

AL REMPEL
"Tilt," "Spine," "In Reverse," "Inside" previously published in *Grain*; "This Summer" previously published on-line in *Reflections on Water*.

ANDREAS SCHROEDER
"Renovating Heaven" is an excerpt from a forthcoming novella by the same name.

MELANIE SIEBERT
"Tundra" previously published in *Martlet*; "Nahanni River, Day 9" previously published in the *Malahat Review*.

Roxanne Willems Snopek
"Two Steps Forward" previously published in *Rhubarb*.

HARRY TOURNEMILLE
"The End of Swinburne" previously published in *Rhubarb*.

K. LOUISE VINCENT
"Walking the Trapline" previously published in *A Room of One's Own*; "When the Dark Work Started" previously published in *The Invention of Birds: the Island Women Poets* (Leaf Press, 2003). In "I Find all Devotion Difficult," the line "The works of all the visionaries have walked away" is Theresa Kishkan's.